THE S_
FOR ORION

The Art of Darkness, Book 1

A Supernatural Adventure

The underworld is closer

than you think

BY KEITH CADOR

Prepared for publication by Karen Perkins
www.karenperkinsauthor.com

As this is my first book and means everything to me, I would like to dedicate it to my beautiful daughter, Jessica Rose Corneby-Robinson, who was born sleeping. I know she's always looking down on me and my family, protecting us. Love you always. X

CONTENTS

An old Cherokee told his grandson:

"My son, there's a battle between two wolves inside us all.

"One is EVIL – it's anger, jealousy, greed, resentment, inferiority, lies and ego.

"The other is GOOD – it's joy, peace, love, hope, humility, kindness and truth."

The boy thought about it and asked, "Grandfather, which wolf wins?"

The old man quietly replied, "The one you feed."

Author unknown

THE SEARCH

FOR ORION

PROLOGUE

Excerpt from The Brunswick Bugle

MORE INFORMATION HAS BEEN RELEASED ABOUT EVENTS AT A LOCAL DERELICT TUNNEL. EYEWITNESSES SPOKE OF POLICE DETAINING SEVERAL PEOPLE AND TWO AMBULANCE CREWS ATTENDING THE INJURED.

DET. CORNEBY SAID IN A STATEMENT:

"I WISH TO CLARIFY THAT THE POLICE ARE DEALING WITH THIS INCIDENT WITH AS MUCH HASTE AS POSSIBLE. HOWEVER, THE EXTREME AND UNIMAGINABLE EVENTS THAT OCCURRED IN THIS VICINITY A WEEK AGO TODAY, CANNOT BE DEALT WITH LIGHTLY. THIS IS NOT ONE SINGLE PIECE OF VILLAINY, BUT A MULTITUDE OF EVILS OVER SEVERAL GENERATIONS."

CHAPTER 1

1990

ANOTHER DAY IN BRUNSWICK

"**M**orning, loser!" yelled a voice, followed by the thump of a smelly sports bag on the desk.

"Marshall!" Olly said, jumping off his chair. "Keep the noise down, you'll get us kicked out."

"All right, keep your hair on, it's only the stupid library . . . anyway, lessons haven't started yet."

"OK, whatever." Olly rolled his eyes.

James Marshall was one of his friends who'd thrashed him on *Goal* on his Nintendo last night. He didn't hang around with him at school too much, as Marshall was always getting into trouble and bunking off. He was usually at the games arcade in town, and held the record for *Street Fighter*.

Marshall and Oliver Webber were thirteen years old and second years at St Aidan's C of E High School. Both boys were confident for their age, especially Marshall, whose posh accent made him sound bullish – an attribute he'd picked up from a private boarding school he used to attend, before being expelled. Although of medium height and build, with short black hair, Marshall did have a distinguishing feature: he had a third nipple. Once the other boys noticed this abnormality in the changing rooms, he was singled out and had to endure various nicknames. This was probably the reason for him having missed so much school: to avoid the other kids bullying him and laughing at him behind his back.

"Knew you were bad at *Goal*, mate, but 5-0?" Marshall boasted. "No wonder you wanted rid of me early!"

"Very funny, mate. I was knackered . . . I'll beat

3

you next time. Anyway, what are you doing up in the library? I didn't realise you could read," Olly asked, breaking out in laughter.

Putting his hand to his mouth, Marshall replied, "Yawn, yawn. Is there ever going to be a day when you're not sarcastic? I found a newspaper cutting, it was lining one of my drawers at home. Thought you might be interested, with liking all those mystery books, but if you're not I'll be off."

Olly was intrigued. "Oh, OK, let's have a look then, but after, will you please leave me in peace?"

With a great sense of importance, Marshall pulled out an old newspaper cutting and lay it on the table for Olly to read:

YOUNG MAN DISAPPEARS IN BRUNSWICK.

ORION HART WAS LAST SEEN ON SATURDAY, WHEN HE SET OFF TO GO FISHING AT THE LAKE IN BRUNSWICK FOREST. HE HAS NOT BEEN SEEN SINCE. HIS WIFE, MELANIE, WITH WHOM ORION HAS A SIX-MONTH-OLD BOY NAMED LEO, IS EXTREMELY WORRIED FOR HIS SAFETY. ORION IS 6FT TALL, OF SLIM BUILD WITH DARK-

BLOND HAIR. HE HAS A DISTINCTIVE BIRTHMARK OF THREE LINES RUNNING DOWN THE SIDE OF HIS NECK. PLEASE GET IN TOUCH WITH THE POLICE ON 0333 269754 IF YOU HAVE INFORMATION.'

"How old is this, mate?" Olly asked.

"Well, the other half of the paper has a date on it, making it eleven years old."

"Oh my God," Olly gasped.

"What's wrong?"

"Don't you realise? His son, Leo . . . he's at our school."

Marshall's eyes lit up. "You're joking, aren't you?"

"No, there's a Leo Hart in the year below. Haven't you seen him? He's a really good footballer," Olly enthused.

The boys sat in the library until the bell went, discussing what to do. Should they mention his father to him? Did he know his father had vanished? Was he even the right Leo Hart? After much deliberation, Olly and Marshall came to the same conclusion – find him at dinner time, confront him and just ask him.

***

At 12:15p.m., as always, the dinner bell rang, and the boys made their way through long corridors into the school yard. Olly and Marshall couldn't have looked any more different as Olly swayed his arms with his jaunty swagger, while Marshall walked very upright with his arms locked straight down his side. Against the far wall they saw a boy kicking a ball.

"There, that's him," Olly said, pointing.

"You sure?"

"Certain. Come on, let's do this."

Making their way through a playground of noisy children, the boys were oblivious to anyone else there. Their eyes were focused on Leo Hart, and nothing was going to distract them.

"Leo, isn't it?" Olly asked with a rare nervousness.

Turning around, a small, blond boy with a neat side parting gave a shy response. "Yeah why? Who are you?"

"I'm Olly and this is Marshall. We're in the year above . . . can we ask you something?"

"What?"

Stepping forward with the newspaper, Marshall said, "Here, read this. We want to know if this is about your dad."

Leo stood, silent with his head bowed, reading the paper cutting. The wind blew across the playground, making the paper flap around and Leo lose his balance. After what seemed like hours, he lifted his head and with tears in his eyes he asked, "Where did you get this?"

"Found it lining one of my chests of drawers at home. I thought it was interesting, so I showed it to Olly 'cause he likes reading about mysteries and stuff like that. That's when he mentioned you were at this school."

Leo sighed, "Well, you've found me."

"Brilliant! So, was he found? Where was he found? Was he OK?" Olly asked, as quizzical as ever.

"Hang on, slow down," Leo replied. "He was never found. No clues, no messages, nothing."

"Oh sorry mate, didn't realise," muttered Olly, embarrassed.

Sitting down on a bench, Leo carried on, "The police told my mum they think he ran away from his problems. My parents were struggling for money at the time, then I came along and my dad just couldn't handle it anymore."

"And you and your mum believe that?" Marshall asked.

"Yes, in the way we believe he's still out there somewhere and not dead. My mum still says that one day he'll come back home. He loved us too much to walk away just because of money problems."

"Let us help you!" exclaimed Olly.

"Don't be daft, it was eleven years ago and anyway, where would we start?"

Putting an arm around him, Marshall said, "Look, what harm can it do? We know he went off to the Brunswick Forest to go fishing . . . we'll do exactly the same."

"But why? Why would you both want to help me? You've never even talked to me before today."

"There's no reason to help, just curiosity, really. Anyway, you got anything else planned this weekend?" Olly beamed.

"This weekend?" said a surprised Leo.

"Why the heck not? I'm in!" Marshall shouted.

"Well OK, I'll tell my mum I'm staying at my friend's house," Leo said, with a hint of excitement. "I better not tell her the truth, though, I don't want to upset her by bringing up the past."

The school bell rang for the children to go back to their classes and Olly and Leo exchanged phone numbers. "I'll ring you later," Olly said.

"OK. Oh and thanks. It means a lot," replied Leo.

"No problem, glad we can help."

Olly and Marshall were so excited about what they'd just found out that they had forgotten which lessons came next. Eventually remembering, they agreed to meet up after school.

The afternoon dragged on as if bathed in treacle. Both boys sat in different classrooms watching every second crawl by on the wall clock. Olly compiled a list of things they might need. Sleeping bags, torches, matches, a compass, first aid kit, Ordnance Survey map, knife, food and drink. He also kept thinking about what would happen if they found a body. How would they react? What would Leo do?

"Olly . . . Olly . . . OLLY!" shouted Mr Lever, the English teacher. "Is there any chance we could have just a few minutes of your attention today please?"

"Sorry, sir, had a late night," Olly quipped.

The rest of the class burst into laughter. "OK, calm down everyone! If you put as much effort into your schoolwork as you do playing those stupid computer games, you'd go far," Mr Lever retorted.

Before Olly could reply, the bell for home time sounded. Throwing his books into his bag he headed to the school gates, eager to meet Marshall.

"Now then, Olly, ready for an adventure?" asked Marshall, jumping on his back.

"Get off, you idiot!" Olly laughed. "Don't get carried away, we might not find anything."

"We will, I'm feeling lucky. Anyway, it's still a weekend camping away from home."

"True, mate, what time shall we meet?"

"How about nine-ish at mine?" Marshall said.

"Yeah that's fine, gives me time to take my dog out first. I'll give Leo a ring when I get home, find out where he lives then we can go and meet him together."

"OK, see you in the morning."

CHAPTER 2

THE ADVENTURE STARTS

Saturday morning arrived with a heavy fog hugging the Yorkshire town of Brunswick. Olly was up bright and early, fighting his sister to be first into the bathroom, while their parents caught up on some much-needed sleep after working a late shift at the local hospital. Olly stood in front of the mirror, yawned and started his usual morning routine. He brushed his teeth then threw a few handfuls of water over his face and hair. He'd never been one for taking time over his appearance, especially his wavy brown hair, which sat on top of his head like a bird's nest (according to his sister). He gave his slim physique a quick blast with deodorant, headed back to his bedroom and put on his usual weekend attire of baggy jeans and a T-shirt displaying his favourite band of the moment.

His bedroom was the highest room in a large Victorian terraced house, as far away as possible from all the noise and disturbances a busy family home brought. Hiding the monotonous magnolia-painted walls, his room was adorned with a mixture of posters from films and, more important to Olly, his favourite bands. He dreamed of someday being in a band himself, standing in front of thousands of crazy fans singing along with him, but this was more of a pipe dream as the only instrument he could play was the trumpet – an interesting choice which he first picked up in junior school and kind of just stuck with, much to his neighbours' annoyance.

Olly set off on a stroll with Madison, his adored golden Labrador. He decided to take her for a quick run through the forest, motivated by the knowledge that he and his friends would be back soon looking for clues to find Orion Hart.

Normally, he would just wander without a care in the world, listening to music on his Sony Walkman and throwing sticks for Madison to chase, but this time his eyes were focused on the ground, hoping to find something connected with the disappearance of Leo's dad. Walking along his normal route, his new-found optimism faded as he noticed nothing looked different to any other day in the woods.

Deciding to head back he shouted, "Come on, Maddy!" He felt nervous as he watched the creeping fog swirl around the trees, until in the distance he saw a golden flash bounding towards him through the mist. "Good girl, come on, let's get you back home."

Once they were back and the dog was drying, Olly topped up her food and water bowls. His parents were working all weekend, so he and his sister were both in charge. His sister, Jess, was eighteen years old and went to the local university. She loved going out and was often partying with her boyfriend, Sam. Olly didn't mind this too much, preferring to stay in most nights listening to music or playing his Nintendo with a few friends.

"Hey, Jess."

"Yes, what do you want?" Jess asked, knowing her brother like the palm of her hand.

"Well, my mates and I are off on a bit of an adventure, so please could you keep an eye on Maddy? I've just taken her out, so she'll be OK till later."

Giving a huge sigh, Jess replied, "Yes that's fine, I've nothing going on this weekend apart from seeing Sam. What are you up to on your adventure?"

"Well I shouldn't really say, but we met this kid in school whose father disappeared when he was a baby and we're going to find out what happened."

"Really?" Jess said, as he grabbed her attention. "Where you off to?"

"Oh, just down the road. He vanished during a fishing trip at the lake in Brunswick Forest."

"Well take care, and make sure you ring home when you see a phone box."

"Don't worry, we'll be fine. I'm off up to Marshall's house now to meet him," said Olly, grabbing his rucksack off the kitchen table.

"OK, promise you'll ring me later to make sure you're all right?"

"Will do . . . that reminds me, I've got to give Leo a call," he said, dashing into the hallway.

He dialled and Leo answered straight away. "Hi, it's Olly, is everything still OK?"

"Yeah fine . . . well, not really mate. A bit scared, to be honest."

"Don't blame you, think I'd be in these circumstances," replied Olly. "We'll call it off if you want?"

"No, it's fine. Once we get going, I'll feel better about it," Leo said. "So, where should we meet?"

"I'm on my way to Marshall's house near the school."

"How about meeting at the white gate at the end of School Lane?" Leo suggested.

"Yeah cool, I know where you mean. We'll be about half an hour."

"Cool, see you both soon."

Half an hour passed, and the three boys met up at the white gate. Marshall turned up in ripped jeans with a black T-shirt and his favourite black, worn leather jacket while Leo came prepared, wearing a waterproof jacket and walking boots.

15

"Nice to see someone's come ready for an adventure," Olly said, grinning at Marshall.

"I'm ready, I've got everything I need in my bag, cheeky."

Leo laughed at his two new friends mocking each other. "Are you both always like this?"

Marshall answered first, "Yes, he's the annoying one who thinks he's funny and I'm the cool, sensible one."

"Ha-ha, you said I was the funny one," Olly joked. "And don't be fooled by his posh accent, Leo, he's rougher than a piece of sandpaper!"

"Yeah, whatever you say," Marshall said, smiling. All three boys laughed and gave one another a hug.

Beyond the lane lay a single farm track stretching into the distance and connecting to the forest. "You ready to do some exploring?" Olly said, with slight trepidation.

"Yeah, I'm feeling better now. Never done anything like this before, how about you?" Leo said, looking at Marshall.

"I've been camping a few times, but mainly with adults. This should be a lot more fun."

Jumping over the gate, Olly said, "Come on guys, let's get going."

Picking up their bags and slinging them over their shoulders, the three boys set off. "So, your dad's got a strange name, do you know anything about it?" Olly asked Leo, trying to make small talk.

"Yeah it's after the star constellation Orion. He was born when there was some planetary alignment within the constellation which was quite a big deal at the time, so he was named after it. My dad carried on the tradition as I was born during an alignment of the Leo constellation."

"Oh, that's cool," Olly said. "My names are boring, even my middle name is Andrew."

"How about you, Marshall?" asked Leo. "Any stories behind your names?"

"Yeah, Marshall," interrupted Olly. "What's your middle name? I've seen a letter G on some of your school books and wondered what it stood for."

Marshall laughed. "Ha, there is no way I'm telling you that, it's an old family name and far too embarrassing."

"OK fair enough, mate, James G Marshall it is,

then," Olly said, laughing with the others.

The boys walked on towards the forest, a slight drizzle starting to fall on their faces.

"Come on lads, I'll race you into the forest, think it's going to chuck it down soon!" Marshall shouted, already ten paces in front of the others.

They chased after him, but then Leo slowed down. "You OK?" Marshall called, puffing for air.

"Think so, just getting a bit nervous of what we might find," Leo said, as the trees at the edge of the forest loomed over them like giants guarding a fortress.

"Don't worry. Your dad went missing a long time ago," Olly said comforting him. "I'd be very surprised if we find anything to upset you, we're only here to see where he disappeared and hopefully find a clue."

"Yeah I understand," agreed Leo.

Striding into the forest, talk soon lessened as they made their way through the undergrowth, their heads bowed to scan the forest floor for any clues. "Are we going the right way?" Marshall asked.

"Yeah," Olly replied. "We're off to the lake. If he was off fishing it makes sense to start looking there."

A slight mist still weaved in and out of the trees, and along with the noise of birds and snapping twigs in the undergrowth, there was a spooky feel to the adventure. "Aren't you scared?" Leo asked, keeping close to Olly.

"No, mate, I'm used to it. I must walk through these woods at least three times a week. Look at that there," Olly said, pointing down at some paw prints in the mud. "They're my dog, Madison's. Told you I know this area."

"We're here!" Marshall said.

The boys ran over to where they could also see the lake. The mist was floating over it and everything was silent. Seeing the other side, they decided to split up and walk round it. Olly and Leo went left while Marshall went right.

"See you in a few minutes, guys, and don't forget to keep looking for clues," Marshall encouraged.

They walked along the edge of the lake, their feet slipping and sticking in the mud. Large tree roots crept down the slopes, ending in the murky waters.

"We're never going to find anything here," Leo moaned.

"Well, it is tough with all this mud about but chin up, we've plenty of time to keep looking," replied Olly. "How's your mum been through all this? Or does she not talk about your dad?"

"She tends to keep everything to herself, probably to protect me more than anything else. We still have the odd picture of my dad up in the house, but as I never knew him 'cause I was too young, she thinks I don't need to know . . . if that makes sense?"

"Yeah I understand. If it ain't broke, then don't fix it. I think that's the right saying."

The three boys carried on around the lake looking everywhere from high up in the trees to low down into the water. They had circled four or five times when a call came out. "Hey guys!" Marshall shouted. "Get yourselves over here."

They ran through the slippery undergrowth as best they could, eventually catching up with Marshall. "You found something, mate?" Olly asked.

His face gleaming, Marshall nodded and opened his hand out to reveal an old locket. "I found it under this tree root. It was a bit muddy, but I've given it a rinse in the lake."

"Wow, it's beautiful," Olly said. "Such good condition, the mud must have preserved it over all these years."

"That's what I thought."

"Have you opened it yet?" Leo asked.

"Yes. Do you want a look?" Marshall said, unclipping the locket, "Is this you as a baby?"

Leo stood shaking, "Yes. Yes, it's me, oh my God, I've got a copy of this picture at home!"

"You know what this means don't you, Leo?" Olly remarked.

Marshall and Leo looked at him with a glazed expression on their faces. "Come on, lads, it means he didn't run off after all. Someone or something took him from this spot, and he dropped the locket in the struggle. He wouldn't plan to disappear and hide a locket, would he?"

"Yeah, suppose you're right," Leo whispered, wiping a tear away from his face.

"Don't be upset," Marshall said. "At least we know we're on the right track."

"I know. Can't believe no one's ever found this locket before now. Apparently, the police were here for days searching the area."

"It was well hidden under the roots. Just call it beginner's luck." Marshall smiled.

"Yeah, we need all the luck we can muster if we're to find Leo's dad," Olly agreed.

The boys continued along the bank, splodging and slipping through the mud, hoping to find more clues. Leo kept the locket safe in his coat, stopping every now and then to take a look. The weather was worsening. Large droplets of rain pierced the still surface of the lake, but the boys weren't fazed. They had found a clue. Nothing was going to make them head home early.

CHAPTER 3

THE SERPENT'S LAIR

"Where should we go now?" Leo asked.

"How about this way?" Marshall said, pointing towards an old embankment.

"Yeah, why not," said Olly, agreeing with him for a change.

"Where does it lead?" Leo asked.

"It just follows down the side of the forest, we walk on here quite a lot as well. It's where the old railway line used to run."

Making their way up the steep slope of the embankment, the boys made their way along the top.

Overgrown with bramble bushes and nettles, the way became precarious and the boys were forced to tread carefully.

"Can't believe this used to be a train line," Leo enthused. "Imagine a train coming along now, we'd have to jump out of the way and roll down the hill."

"Not really." Marshall laughed. "It's probably about a hundred years since the last train came along here, so I think we're pretty safe."

"I found an old motorbike round here once," remembered Olly. "It was just there between those trees. God knows how it got there."

"Maybe it had to swerve out of the way of a train," Marshall said, laughing.

"Ha-ha, very funny," Leo said. "What did you do with it?"

"Me and Jess managed to get it home, then we contacted the police, just in case it was stolen. When we found out nobody was missing it, we gave it to my dad to restore. He loves bikes and it's a bit of a hobby for him. In fact, he's still doing it up now."

"What does your dad do for a living, Olly?" Leo asked.

"He's a nurse at the local hospital. My mum is too. They're both working all weekend, so I told them I'm camping at Marshall's house."

"What about your parents, Marshall?" Leo asked again.

"Well, my mum works at the local supermarket, but my dad passed away when I was young."

"Sorry to hear that. Looks like we have something in common: growing up without a father."

"Suppose you're right. My mum's remarried and it's nice having a father figure around again. It was a long time ago and I can't remember my dad anyway, I've only got photos. He was meant to be a great person though, so I've been told."

The boys continued along the embankment even though it was becoming more and more overgrown. They used long sticks like swords, chopping down the nettles and brambles in front of them like knights slaying their enemies. Eventually the embankment flattened out and they were on level ground again. Still slashing their swords, something emerged through the overgrowth.

"Look, lads," Marshall gasped. "It's a tunnel."

"Cool," Leo replied. "Didn't know this was here, suppose where there's a train track there's going to be a tunnel."

"I know what this is, it's The Serpent's Lair," Olly announced.

"The Serpent's Lair! What's that?" Leo muttered.

"I heard about it from the lads at school," Olly replied. "It's an old railway tunnel that went under the town but got abandoned a long time ago. Some kids named it after that Acorn Electron game – apparently, they heard strange noises coming from inside. Some of my friends have been in it since though and said there's nothing in there, apart from the pitch black and mud."

"So, what should we do?" Leo asked.

"Not too sure," Olly replied.

The entrance was boarded up by large, metal doors which over time had rusted and weakened. Fixed on to the doors was a sign which read: *KEEP OUT. TRESPASSERS WILL BE PROSECUTED.* To the boys, this message meant: *COME ON IN AND EXPLORE.*

"We've come this far," Marshall pointed out.

"There's no harm in having a little look."

"OK, let's do this," Olly said. "Get your torches out."

The boys dug deep into their rucksacks and pulled out their torches. "Hey, Leo stop it!" Olly shouted as Leo pointed the torch straight into his eyes. "Save your batteries, we might be in there a while."

Marshall was the first one to squeeze through a small opening which must havc been where other children had kicked through the rusted metal. "Come on, guys," he said as he got off his knees inside the tunnel.

"We're coming," Olly replied, helping Leo through the small opening.

"Wow!" Leo said shining his torch in front of him. "It's massive."

Olly made his way into the tunnel last and stood up with the others. "Are you two still sure about this? I mean you're not scared or anything are you?"

"Well it's a bit scary but as long as we're together we'll be OK." Leo shivered.

"I'm fine," Marshall said. "A bit of darkness doesn't scare me; it's the ghosts you have to look out for."

"Stop trying to frighten him," Olly said.

"I'm just joking," Marshall sniggered. "The scariest things in here are probably the rats."

The three boys walked slowly down the tunnel. It was very wet underfoot as the roof had large cracks with water seeping through, the droplets echoing as they fell to the ground. The old railway track was still there, helping them keep their footing. The sound of scurrying rats could be heard as they raced over the line.

"Right, lads, turn your torches off," Olly said.

"Are you crazy?" Leo gasped.

Laughing, Olly replied, "Don't worry, I'm keeping mine on, I just don't want us to run out of batteries that's all." Moving his torch around the vast brick archway he exclaimed, "This is amazing, guys. It must have taken them years to build."

"Wait, what's that?" Leo asked. "Move the torch back that way."

Olly moved the light back to the centre of the roof. "Er, you know what they are," Marshall said, pointing at a large dark shape. "Bats . . . and lots of them."

"Now I'm scared," Leo said, hiding behind Olly.

"Don't worry. They're probably more scared of us than we are of them. As long as we keep the noise down, we'll be fine," Olly replied.

Trudging onward, each step seemed to get harder and harder as the water and mud grew deeper. Olly was swaying his torch from side to side when he saw something reflecting the light, close to the side wall. "Hey guys, wait on, I think I've spotted something," he said as he wandered over to the wall and reached down into the water.

"What is it?" Marshall asked.

"An old fishing reel," replied Olly.

"Is it your dad's?" Marshall asked Leo.

"I've no idea, but if it was how did it get down here?"

"Who knows? But if he was taken, this is a good place to hide someone."

"OK Marshall," Olly said. "Stop making things up, you're giving him false hope."

"I'm not at all. First, we find his locket, and now you find a fishing reel which could be his. I tell you we're on the right track."

Olly wiped the fishing reel clean with his sleeve,

"You know, he may be on to something, look."

He showed Leo an engraving on the reel which read: *TO ORION HART – CHAMPION FISHERMAN.*

"It's his, it's my dad's!" Leo shouted. "He must be in here somewhere, don't you reckon?"

Olly wasn't too sure. "You know, a lot of kids have been in this tunnel before and nothing's ever been found. Whoever took him must have taken him somewhere else."

"But at least we're another step closer to finding him," Marshall said. "Come on, let's carry on, this tunnel can't go on forever."

The boys continued on, but there was no more sign of any more clues. Olly kept his torch shining in front of him, whistling one of his favourite songs to break the silence.

"At least whistle a good tune," Marshall suggested. "Something a bit rockier and upbeat."

"Where do you think we are, Wembley? Hold on a minute, I'll just get my drum kit out of my rucksack," Olly said.

"I take it you both like music, then?" Leo asked.

"Well, I do," replied Olly. "He just likes loud noise."

"Very funny, it's called rock music. You'll understand one day."

"We'll lend you some tunes when we get out of here and you can make up your own mind who likes the best music," said Olly.

"Sounds good, I'm not really into music at the moment, so I'll look forward to that, although it might be a while, though, this is going on for ever." Leo sighed, and his shoulders slumped forward.

"Hang on, I think there may be light at the end of the tunnel, if you pardon the pun," Olly said. "Look at the beam of light ahead, it's getting wider. We must be reaching the end."

All three boys walked faster, making bigger splashes through the water until they came to a wall of boulders reaching the ceiling. They were covered with graffiti where other kids must have hung out; empty cans and bottles were strewn across the wet floor.

"I guess that's the end of that, then," Leo muttered. "The end of the line."

"You've cracked it, Leo," Olly said, with a blast of enthusiasm.

"What do you mean?"

"Well, it's not the end of the line . . . it carries on through the boulders."

The boys looked for any holes in the rocks where they could crawl through. They also tried to force stones through to the other side, but to no avail. The wall was solid. "Well that's just great," Marshall said angrily, picking up a glass bottle then throwing it as hard as he could against the tunnel wall. "We're never going to find him now."

"Sshhh, Marshall, can you hear that?" Olly whispered. "It's coming from back there."

They all looked back down the tunnel as Olly shone his torch. Coming towards them were hundreds of bats, startled into flight when Marshall had smashed the beer bottle. "Oh no!" Leo shouted.

"Everyone get down!" bellowed Olly.

The bats thundered towards them, screeching and flapping wildly as the boys clung on to each other for dear life. "I'm scared," Leo said, shaking.

"Stay close to me, I think I've noticed something," Olly said.

"What's happening?" Marshall said, feeling forced to open his eyes.

Olly shone his torch upwards. "Look . . . the bats are disappearing but they're not going back up the tunnel. They must have found a gap in the rocks. Let's wait till all the bats have gone and see if we can get up there."

The bats flew off, leaving the three boys free to climb the wall. Marshall was first and Olly shone the torch to help him. Some rocks were protruding which Marshall used as steps. He also used a large stick he'd found, to dislodge some stones higher up. "Right, I can't go any further now. My head's touching the roof."

"Can you see a gap at all?" Olly asked.

"Not sure, throw me your torch."

Olly threw it, making it spin like a lightsabre slicing through the air.

"Yes, I see a hole," Marshall said, pointing the torch. "It's not too big but I can loosen some more stones."

He bashed away at them with his stick. Fragments fell down, nearly hitting the others on their heads.

"Any luck? Before you kill us both," Olly asked.

"Sorry about that, lads, but there was quite a bit to clear. Think we'll be able to squeeze through now," Marshall said with his body already halfway through.

"OK, we'll follow you up, mate."

One at a time, the boys climbed up through the small hole Marshall had created, then climbed down the other side. Olly made his way down last.

"I told you two not to waste your torch batteries, turn them off."

"They are off," came the resounding reply.

Turning around in astonishment, Olly could see the continuation of the tunnel but this time it was illuminated. "What are they?" he asked, pointing up to the ceiling.

"Not too sure," Marshall said. "Never seen anything like that on any nature programme before."

Above the boys, hundreds of small creatures were emanating an orange glow from their bodies. They looked like grasshoppers, and the roof appeared to be moving. "Are we safe?" Leo asked.

"Think so," Olly replied. "Anyway, at least we won't need our torches while they're above us."

"Hey," said Leo. "Look what I've found. It's the rest of my dad's fishing gear. We're definitely on the right track now. Whoever took it must have dumped it all."

"You're right. Whoever it was didn't want people to find it, that's for sure," Olly said. "I've got to admit you're being so brave about all this. I'd be a quivering wreck."

"Just hasn't sunk in yet, that's all. Still can't believe what we've found down here," he said, with his arm on Marshall's shoulder.

"This place is amazing," Marshall beamed. "It looks like new."

The tunnel was a complete contrast to the one on the other side of the wall. It was dry with no mud on the ground, the track shining from the reflection of the glowing creatures.

"This is crazy," Leo said, looking ahead down the tunnel. "Where does it go?"

"Don't know," Olly replied. "But I don't think many people have been down here. Not since they stopped using it anyway."

"What else do you know about The Serpent's Lair then, Olly?" Marshall asked.

"Not a lot, mate, just what kids at school said, that it's a dark, wet tunnel. They can't have been as far as this anyway, they'd have said something."

Just then a large noise echoed down the tunnel. "What was that?" Leo said, moving between Olly and Marshall.

"Not sure, hopefully not a serpent," replied Marshall. "It's probably some truck going over the top of the tunnel, there'll be loads of roads going over here. Anyway, let's carry on walking. It should be a doddle now we can see where we're going."

The three boys continued their journey, feeling slightly more anxious than before. Marshall turned to Leo. "What happens if we find your dad? Have you thought about it?"

"Haven't stopped thinking about it to be honest, I don't really know. If we find him, he'll be dead, but at least me and my mum will know for sure what happened to him, instead of just wondering."

"We're both here for you, Leo," Olly said. "We won't let you see anything that'll upset you. Anytime you want to go back just say, OK?"

"Thanks, both of you. I just want to find out what really happened to my dad."

As they kept walking, they noticed the light was growing dimmer, making it harder to see. The glowing insects above them were diminishing. Olly got his torch out and pointed it towards the few remaining ones. "Wonder what they are?" he asked himself. "They seem to give off warmth as well, it's definitely a bit colder now than it was when there were loads of them above us."

Leo, who was walking to the side of the train track, suddenly tripped over. "What the heck is that?"

Olly shone his torch over to where Leo had fallen. "Wow!" he said. "Look what you've come across. It's a platform, a proper train platform."

"This is unbelievable," Marshall said, jumping up on to the platform and taking out his own torch. "Look, there's a waiting room and a signal box."

"Cool," replied Olly. "Do you think anyone knows about this? This is a right find."

"I'm not sure anyone knows this is here," Leo replied. "It all looks old but brand new, if you know what I mean?"

"I understand," Olly nodded. "Looks like it was built a long time ago, but no one's ever used it."

Leo grabbed a torch from his rucksack and all three boys explored around the station to see if they could find any clues. "Look, the station name," Olly said pointing. "It's Brunswick Station."

The name was written in gold over a purple background and stood at the beginning of the platform. The waiting room was further along, also painted in gold and purple, with two arched windows filled with stained glass. Inside six seats were covered in brown leather. Pictures above showed the town of Brunswick in all its splendour, and against the far wall stood a grandfather clock – with a pair of gas lights hanging on either side.

"Thinking about it," Leo said. "I'm sure my history teacher mentioned Brunswick Station once during a talk about Brunswick in the Victorian age. He said they built it to ease congestion in the town, but it was closed down in the 1950s due to money problems."

"Well it looks like someone's been cleaning it up since then because it's spotless," Olly said.

"Yeah you're right. Something's been going on down here."

Olly checked out the waiting room while Marshall

inspected the signal box. Leo felt a bit tired, so he rested in one of the comfy chairs, chatting to Olly. "So how long have you been friends with Marshall?" he asked.

"I wouldn't call it a friendship as such, I just know him from my year at school. He sometimes pops round mine to play computer games as well. He seems a good lad, though he's got some anger issues. He got expelled from one school and once got suspended from ours for shouting at a teacher, but he's always been OK with me. It must be hard growing up without his dad, as you well know."

"Yeah it's not easy," Leo shrugged. "But I don't know anything different. My mum's brought me up well."

"Hey you guys!" Marshall bellowed, leaning out of the signal box window. "Have you found anything yet?"

"No, nothing," Olly shouted back. "What's it like up there?"

"It's so cool, it's like brand new, but I can't see any clues."

"Have a look over into the water tank if you can," Olly suggested.

"OK, will do."

Marshall pushed his body as far as he could out of the signal box window, leaning over and down into the tank, "No, can't see anything but I can't reach over enough to see inside all of it."

"No problem," Olly sighed. "It was worth a look."

Marshall climbed down from the signal box and back on to the platform, "Come on then, let's move on!"

Olly and Leo made their way out of the waiting room to join Marshall. Slowly they walked along the platform, frustrated at not finding any more clues about Leo's dad.

"What was that?" Leo said, grabbing Olly's hand.

"What?" Marshall replied.

"I heard something move in there," Leo said, pointing to the water tank.

"There's nothing in there, I just checked. It was probably a rat running about, don't worry."

Walking over to the tank, Olly put his hands over the edge and pulled himself up, "Hey Leo!" he said, straining to keep in position. "Get on Marshall's back and shine your torch in here for me."

Jumping on to Marshall, Leo reached his arm over the tank, lighting it up. "I see something," Olly beamed. "It's a small box, but it keeps moving."

"This is weird, I'm getting freaked out now," Leo said, trembling. "Anyway Marshall, thought you said there was nothing in there?"

"Thought there wasn't."

Olly interrupted, "OK you two let's stop that. We need to stick together. Marshall! Put him down and give me a hand to get in this tank."

Putting his hands together, he pushed up Olly's foot, lifting him into the tank. The object that he'd heard was still shuffling about.

"Should I pick it up, lads?" Olly asked, prowling around it as if it were a deadly snake.

"Yes!" Leo shouted. "I want to see it."

Olly leant over and reached for the box. "Wow, wait till you see this," he said, putting it in his rucksack and clambering back out of the tank. "Right guys, look at this."

He pulled out a cube-shaped object, covered in carved symbols. The box was extremely heavy for its size, suggesting it was made from some sort of metal.

41

Around it ran a bone-coloured inlay, suggesting a possible opening.

"Does it come apart?" Leo enquired.

"Not sure," Olly replied, trying to prise the cube open. "It's not budging. I'll try turning it, might be screwed on."

Olly tried repeatedly but the cube wouldn't open. "Pass it here," Leo said, taking it from Olly's grasp. "Hey, these markings . . . I've seen these before. They're hieroglyphics; it's what ancient Egyptians used to communicate with."

"What's it doing in a water tank in a tunnel under Brunswick, then?" Olly said.

Marshall interrupted, "Who knows, think you should just put it back where you found it, mate. We're here to find Leo's dad not to mess with Egyptian artefacts."

"Yes I know, but this might be a clue to find his dad," Olly said, pulling a face.

Rubbing his sleeve over it to get rid of the mud, Leo got a better look at the symbols. "We studied this at school," he said. "Each picture is a word or phrase. Just give me a minute to think about this."

Suddenly the cube jumped out of his hands. Reaching up, he caught it again, holding it tight. "This is crazy, what the heck is it?" Leo asked.

"No idea, but it wants to get away that's for sure," Marshall replied.

Olly stood close to Leo, shining a torch and waiting for Leo to translate the symbols.

"Right . . . I think I know what it says on the lid." Leo said.

The others stood back while Leo held the cube out at arm's length and read the words out loud:

"RELEASE THE SPIRIT FROM THIS TOMB, HEAVEN IS CLOSING, YOU MUST GO SOON."

On finishing the phrase, the cube once again jumped out of his hand, this time landing on the floor. The three boys stood back, keeping close to one another as the box rattled around. "I'm scared, what should we do?" Leo stammered, clinging on to Olly.

"We should run!" Marshall quipped.

"No!" Olly replied. "We stay, this might be a clue. Anyway, I've got a feeling this is only the beginning of our adventure to find Orion Hart. We must stay strong and together. OK?"

"Yeah, all right," Marshall said.

The boys watched the cube, still shuffling about on the floor, when it stopped and a bright light appeared from the white line down the centre. The lid began to turn, making a noise like fingernails being dragged down a chalkboard. With each turn the light grew brighter and brighter until . . . with a loud bang, the lid shot off straight up into the air, hitting the roof and falling back down again.

A beam of white light streamed from the box, forcing the boys to turn around and cover their eyes. Hesitantly, they turned back. As their eyes adjusted to the light, they removed their fingers one at a time, to see what was in front of them.

CHAPTER 4

1950

IN THE BEGINNING

Brunswick was a thriving spa town, recovering well from the destruction of the Second World War which had ended five years before. Royalty frequently visited the town, especially its Turkish Baths, where they could taste the famous medicinal waters that brought tourists flocking. The large exhibition hall was made from giant panes of glass and overlooked the beautiful Brunswick Gardens. Numerous shows were held there throughout the year, including flower and art shows. During the

45

previous year, the Great Northern Exposition had opened its doors to the people of Brunswick, allowing inventors and scientists to showcase their future technologies.

In charge of these grand events was George Bumble, a very likeable gentlemen and a well-known figure in the community. He was of stout build with a full, white beard, making him very easy to recognise in a crowded room. He was born and bred in Brunswick, only leaving his beloved town to fight in the First World War, where he crossed the English Channel to fight in Belgium.

A proud Englishman, he always wore his campaign medal and never shied away from telling people his war stories, 'They were the worst years, but also the best years of my life,' is how he would always start his stories.

One of the events he organised was the annual Bankers' Ball, where all the banking dignitaries from the region gathered to celebrate their work whilst raising money for charities. It was at this event that George Bumble first met Drake Golding. Drake was very different to George, not just in appearance –

being clean shaven with dark-brown hair combed back – but in his work ethic. He had grown up in Brunswick and was five years younger than George, making him miss out on a call up to the First World War.

He moved to the city to study finance and had been brought up to believe that you have to fight for everything in life, not to trust anyone, and to look after number one; i.e. yourself. Drake attended many charitable events, but seemed to be there for the free food and drink rather than to open his bulging wallet.

At the Bankers' Ball, Drake sat at the top table with his beloved wife Lillian, along with their son, Charles, and his wife Cynthia – who were enjoying their first night out since becoming proud parents to two beautiful twin boys. George Bumble kept the drinks flowing and the conversation lively. Although their characters were very different, they all seemed to hit it off brilliantly.

It was at one of these events that George invited Drake to join a unique club he was part of, called Art of Darkness. Here members would talk about and get involved in anything from black magic to searching for mythical creatures and legends. Their last trip had involved going down to Cornwall to find out about the myth of King Arthur. Drake eagerly accepted George's invitation.

Many years passed with Drake often joining George at the Art of Darkness club, hidden away below an old snooker hall in a run-down area of Brunswick. Inside was a well-stocked bar and gentlemanly décor including leather seats and oak tables. The bookcases were stacked high with tomes detailing stories about ghosts, mythical creatures and magic that members had collated over the years.

The club had about twenty members including Harold Lightbottom, local councillor; Archibald Griffin, archaeologist and founder of the club; and Gerald Sloane, who was an old school friend of Drake. All had sworn never to use any of the learned dark arts outside the club.

One evening Drake and George were alone in the club. "So, George," said Drake. "Have you heard about the Brunswick underground?"

"You mean Brunswick Station?" replied George. "Yes, I have. Such a shame. I was speaking to Harold Lightbottom just the other day about this. They're going to close it don't you know?"

"Yes, I had heard. What happens to it after it closes?"

"Nothing's been mentioned yet, but it's such a waste. A lot of time and money went into that station."

"So, why is it closing down?"

"Think it's just a lack of use." George sighed. "More and more people are buying cars, you see. Anyway, why all the questions?"

Drake put his single malt whisky down on the table. "I've got an idea . . . an idea which involves you."

Drake's plans involved a train ride through the tunnel, stopping at Brunswick Station. Passengers could then enter an elaborate maze or labyrinth, passing through different rooms to find their way out.

"You seemed to have found yourself a money

spinner there, Drake," George said, eager to find out more.

"Why, thank you," said Drake. "But I need you on board. I've known you for . . . well it must be about five years now. I trust you as a friend, and I'd like to trust you as a business partner. After all, you know the right people involved in entertainment to help with designing the labyrinth."

"Well you're right there, I do have a lot of contacts. But how can we afford it?"

"Don't worry about that, I'm a banker," Drake said with a wink. "If I can't find the money, no one can." He picked up his whisky, knocked it back and left the room, leaving George to reflect on this new opportunity.

Within weeks the last train had pulled out of Brunswick Station. With the official closure, Drake was ready to pounce. He made the rail company an offer they couldn't refuse, especially with them losing so much money in the last few years.

Drake arranged dozens of meetings with the appropriate authorities and got the results he had wanted – as he always did.

"Well, first things first," Drake said, after meeting George at the club. "We are now the owners of the Brunswick tunnel."

"What great news!" George said, giving his colleague a hug. "Now for the hard work, my friend."

"Yes, it's going to take a few years but I'm sure it'll be worth it in the end, I've got a lot of money riding on this," Drake replied.

The newly formed business partnership met as often as they could, despite their own work commitments. Each time they'd have new ideas to add to their project and things progressed well. They had decided to keep the train platform and track, as it was a fun way of getting into the tunnel, but they still had to find a place for the labyrinth rooms. The only way was to break through the wall of the tunnel beyond the platform.

George asked Ron Higgins for advice. Ron, a member of the club, was an explosives expert, and they met at the station one afternoon to get things underway.

About fifty holes were drilled into the cave wall, then sticks of dynamite lodged inside them. George was concerned by this, as he thought it might also destroy most of the platform, but Ron convinced him it was a good idea.

The three men stood a hundred yards back down the tunnel and watched as the explosives detonated. A large boom echoed around them, followed by a large, suffocating dust cloud. Chunks of rock fell from above, narrowly avoiding George.

"I knew this was a bad idea," George said, holding his hands over his head.

"Don't worry. Let's see what's happened to the wall. We can tidy this up later," Drake replied.

Ron retreated from the tunnel whilst the two gentlemen walked past the platform, waving away the thick cloud of ash and smoke. As the cloud dispersed, they could see what was left.

"It's perfect," George said, looking at the new archway.

"You're right, and not one bit of damage to the station."

They walked up to look through, and stood in awe at what they saw.

"What have we found here?" Drake said.

"Not sure. It looks amazing though," George said, putting a comradely arm around his business partner.

Visible through the archway was a large floor with an opening at the opposite end.

"Come on, Drake," George said. "Let's wander over to that cave and explore."

Just as they made their way through the archway, the floor in front of them rumbled.

"Here, grab my hand!" Drake shouted, stretching out his arm to pull George towards him and back into the safety of the archway. The floor in front of them fell in one huge mass, crashing from on high and creating another dust cloud.

"What on earth's happening?" Drake said.

"Not sure, might be that the explosion has weakened the rocks. We'd better be careful!"

As the dust fell, they looked across to the cave, but instead of looking across solid ground as before, a gigantic chasm stretched over fifty feet wide.

"What now? We can't get to the cave. All the money I've put into this project, and all we've got is a train ride to an archway," Drake moaned.

"Just hold your horses one second," George replied. "Setbacks like this are going to happen, especially with something we haven't tried before. But it's how we come back with a solution that matters."

"Go on then, solve this setback," Drake said, as he patted the dust off his overcoat.

"I know!" George said. "We'll build a bridge, it'll be perfect. Just think, the train will bring them into the tunnel, they get off at the platform and walk through the archway, then they cross a bridge. All that before they even start into the labyrinth of caves."

Drake smiled. "This is why I wanted you as a business partner, with ideas like this. It sounds perfect."

Turning around, the two men saw a figure running up to them. "Drake, Drake!" Ron shouted. "It's your wife, Lillian."

"What's happened to her?" Drake asked.

"Nothing's happened to her, but she's outside the tunnel crying. Please hurry!"

Drake and George ran to the opening of the tunnel

to see what the matter was. Lillian rushed up to Drake and hugged him. "I've got some awful news," she said. "It's Charles, Cynthia and the boys."

"What about them?"

"They've been involved in a car crash."

CHAPTER 5

LIGHT AT THE END OF THE TUNNEL

Six months had passed since the death of Drake and Lillian's son and daughter-in-law. George had kept in touch with Drake as much as he could, despite the numerous changes in Drake's life. Charles and Cynthia may have passed away, but their twin sons, Lance and Victor had survived the horrific crash, leaving them as orphans. Drake had no other option but to take them in as his own.

He decided to retire from his banking duties, giving him plenty of free time to bring up the children. He also knew he was going to make money from the Brunswick Tunnel venture.

While Drake and his wife were organising their lives around the new arrivals, George carried on with the planning and building of the labyrinth, concentrating on the bridge. It was constructed of wooden slats held together by rope, which swayed from side to side as you walked along it, adding to the excitement. The builders even finished off a few of the labyrinth rooms, with the idea of the public having to complete challenges in each room before entering the next one.

One Sunday morning, Drake had organised to meet up with George at the tunnel to see how things were progressing. It was easier to concentrate and imagine new ideas without builders banging their tools and the diggers digging. They walked up the long tunnel, with George shining his torch ahead of them, when they reached the platform.

"This looks fabulous!" George remarked. "It's so clean."

"It better be, the wages we're paying these builders," moaned Drake.

"Are you feeling all right? I know you've been through a lot these last few months."

"I'm fine, just want this place sorted. I'm not making too much money now I've retired,"

The platform had been repainted to the highest quality and the seats in the waiting room re-covered with the finest leather. There were even golden oil lamps attached to the signal box.

"Wow! Look, Drake," said George, shining his torch towards the top of the archway. Carved in the rock was the word: *LABYRINTH*.

"Yes, that does look good. Come on, let's go through," Drake said, showing the first sign of excitement.

The archway led straight to the rope bridge connecting them to the first of the labyrinth caves. "Is this safe?" George asked.

"We'll soon find out," Drake replied, his foot already pressing down on one of the wooden slats.

Taking one step at a time, they crept across the creaky, swaying bridge, trying their best not to look down into the depths of the chasm.

George groaned. "I think they could have made this a bit stronger; it can hardly take my weight."

"Don't worry, George, it's as safe as houses. These

bridges are meant to sway and creak. Anyway, I'm not putting any more money into this."

Once they reached the other side, they saw a sign.

YOU ARE NOW ENTERING THE LABYRINTH.
BE MINDFUL WHERE YOU STEP.
THERE'S ONLY ONE WAY OUT.
IF YOU DARE.

"Right then," George said. "Shall we try out a few of these rooms?"

"I think so, even I'm getting excited."

Both men walked to the first cave. Above the entrance was a rhyme:

IN THE MAZE YOU MUST GO.
THE CLOCK IS TICKING, DON'T BE SLOW.

"Oh yes," George said. "This room has yet to be completed. It hasn't got the timing mechanism installed yet, so no need to rush, we won't get trapped inside."

On entering, they were met by a maze of glass and

mirrors. They felt their way around each corner, occasionally banging against the glass panels. It was very confusing with only the torchlight to guide them, but with more luck than judgement, they reached the end and through to the next cave.

"If this is anything to go by, the people of Brunswick will be in for a real treat," George said, a large grin appearing out of his bushy white beard.

Drake agreed. "Even for an old man like me that was enjoyable."

Another rhyme greeted them at the next cave:

DON'T LOOK DOWN, THE PATH IS CLEAR.
WILL YOUR NERVES CONTROL THE FEAR?

Before them a narrow walkway spanned no wider than one of George's shoes. It twisted for a hundred yards like a giant snake. Either side was a drop to a huge pool of water so one slip would get you seriously wet.

"Right then, George, age before beauty," Drake said, pointing the way.

"Very funny, my friend," George laughed. "I'll go

first but don't rush me; I've just had these clothes washed!"

They made their way across the walkway, each secretly hoping that the other person would fall in.

"You don't think these are too easy, do you?" Drake asked.

"No, not at all. Remember there will be a lot of children coming here and they'll be scared at the thought of crossing this and falling into the water."

"Yes, I suppose you're right."

"So, what have we got here?" George asked, looking up at the next rhyme above the third cave entrance.

PLEASE BE QUICK ACROSS THIS WEB,
DON'T WAKE THE SPIDER,
IT'S NOT BEEN FED.

"Well this looks interesting," Drake said with a smile.

Inside, a web spanned the whole room. "Looks like we might have to get down on our hands and knees for this one," George said.

"Ha-ha, and look at that," Drake said, pointing to

the far corner of the web where a giant fake spider perched.

"My, my. We'd be in a lot of trouble if that was real. I'm too old for running now."

Both men got down on their hands and knees and crawled across the web, spanning their bodies like spiders. There was also a small drop to the water below in case anyone fell through the web.

"This is tiring," Drake said.

"I know," George puffed. "But enjoyable. I think that's as far as the builders have got. There's still a long way to go before any of this will be open to the public."

"Yes, I realise that," agreed Drake. "There are so many caves to transform, at this rate we won't be open even in two years. I must have a word with the builders to speed up their efforts."

"Well I'm sure they're doing their best, but if you'd think that would help?"

"Yes, I do!" Drake said.

Alone, Drake and George decided to continue their exploration. One cave led to another, each corner unveiling more caves. They couldn't believe what they were seeing. There were stalactites and stalagmites so old they met in the middle. The caves would be a big attraction just as they were, without the added excitement of the labyrinth.

"I say, Drake, people would pay good money to come and see this, there's nothing like it around these parts. Not that I'm aware of anyway."

Drake's eyes widened. "I was just thinking that. All that income without having to spend more on those puzzle rooms."

"Money, money, money, is that all you think about? We've just discovered some of the best caves in England and all you can think of is money."

"Money makes the world go around and I don't want to fall off if it stops," Drake replied.

"Ha-ha, I'll never change you, will I?"

They carried on walking, trying their best to remember the way they had entered, when George grabbed Drake's arm. "Stop!" he shouted.

"What?"

George pointed his torch down at their feet. In front of them was a large drop. "Not sure we can go much further than this, it looks dangerous," he said, moving his torch around, looking for a way out of their predicament. Drake saw something glisten in the distance at the bottom of the slope.

"Can you see that, George?"

"What? Where?"

"Over there, there's something reflecting off the torch light."

"It's probably just rats' eyes."

"No, it's bigger than a rat, let's try and get down to have a closer look," Drake said.

Holding each other's arms, they tentatively made their way down, zigzagging due to the steepness. When they reached the bottom and George once again shone the torch, the reflection was even brighter. Both men walked forward towards the light and as they did so, they could see it came from a small cave with a low opening. Drake got down on his knees, followed by George, and they both shuffled their way through the entrance.

"Switch your torch on, George, I can't see a thing."

"I can't, its stopped working!" George said, bashing it on the ground.

"Pass it here, I'll try and tighten it."

After a few minutes of fumbling about in the dark the torch came to life. "Oh my goodness!" both men said in unison.

"I don't believe it," Drake said.

The torch had illuminated a cave and revealed walls adorned with crystals, diamonds, gold and many other minerals.

"This is amazing," George said. "Millions of years must have passed for the rocks to form these precious stones."

"And just think, it's all ours," Drake replied.

George turned to Drake, "Don't be daft. This is the find of the century. The treasure belongs to the town of Brunswick."

"Me being daft?" Drake retorted. "We bought this tunnel fair and square, whatever's in here is ours."

"Yes, we bought the tunnel, Drake, all this is beyond that. We blew through the walls, remember?"

"Yes, I do remember. But you didn't say all these caves should be the property of Brunswick before, yet as soon as we find some treasure, you change your mind."

George shook his head, "I don't believe you,

Drake, all these precious stones would bring so much money to the town and I'm sure we'd still do very well out of it."

"I don't want to do well out of it, I want to have it all," Drake said, thumping the wall of the cave. "Nobody knows it's here apart from us, we could take what we want, sell it and never worry about money again."

"I don't worry about money anyway," George replied, as he got back down on his knees to make his way out. "This is not ours and as soon as we get out of here, the town of Brunswick will hear the good news."

Drake was enraged. "I want what is mine! If you don't want it, then you won't leave these caves alive."

George turned his head around to see Drake coming at him holding a large rock. "Don't do it!" he pleaded. "You'll never get away with it."

"Well, who's to know? I'll close the tunnel and take all the treasure."

"I won't let you. If you kill me, I'll make sure you never get your hands on it."

This angered Drake even more. "You fool,

Bumble!" he shouted, as he brought his arm around and smashed the rock on the poor man's head.

George fell forward on to the ground, his hands clutching the crown of his bleeding head.

"Let's see you stop me now then," Drake said, followed by a callous laugh.

George spoke with a weak, frail voice. "You forget about how long I've been going to the Art of Darkness. I know the afterlife; I've spoken to the dead. Being alive is not your whole life. When your body dies, your spirit lives on and puts right other people's wrongs. Until then your spirit cannot rest."

"Absolute rubbish!" Drake replied. He picked up the same stone again and . . . George Bumble lay motionless, face down on the cave floor. "Let's see what your afterlife thinks about that, then."

Blood seeped from the crown of George Bumble's head, surrounding his body. Drake stood over him, waiting for some movement, but George Bumble was dead.

Drake pushed the body to the side wall and contemplated what to do next. He prised George's torch from his hand and made his way out of the jewelled room, leaving the body behind. Making his way to the bottom of the steep slope he began the ascent. He found it hard to climb back up as his shoes kept slipping on the loose rocks. The quicker he went the less progress he seemed to make. After a huge struggle he managed to reach the top, when he heard a familiar voice. "Drake . . . Drake."

"Who's there?" he said.

"It's me."

Drake looked up and pointed his shaking torch. In front of him was the ghostly figure of George Bumble. "Aarrgghhh!"

"Mwhahahaha!" boomed the ghost. "You think you got rid of me just like that? I told you I would be back."

Drake faltered, nearly crashing down the steep slope he'd just climbed. "What do you want from me?" he said.

"I said I'd never let you have the treasure and I, unlike you, will keep my word!"

Drake couldn't believe what he was seeing. He had talked and read about ghosts at the Art of Darkness club for many years, but to see one in real life shook him to the core. An immense, loud, screeching roar then filled the cave, making the walls shake and crumble.

"If I were you, I'd run and never come back to these caves," boomed the ghost. "This place will be haunted with demons from the underworld, preventing you from getting your filthy, greedy hands on those jewels down there."

The screeching continued and grew louder and louder. Looking back down the slope, Drake saw a large fireball shooting out from another cave. Heavy footsteps could also be heard squelching in the mud and the rocks below. Drake turned to George Bumble's ghost and spoke with terror in his voice, "Is that what I think it is?"

"I told you to run, didn't I? No? Then meet Hornbeam."

"Hornbeam? What's that?"

"Hornbeam the dragon, the new guardian of these caves. Along with the other creatures of the underworld I have summoned, he will stop you from getting your hands on the treasure."

Drake ran back towards the maze of caves. "There

will be a way to get the treasure!" he shouted. "I'll be back."

He ran as fast as an ageing man could do, desperately trying to remember his way out. The noise of Hornbeam echoed around the walls, bursts of light filling the caverns like forked lightning on a stormy night. Drake saw the completed labyrinth rooms and headed straight for them. He heard the ghost's voice again: "Get out, get out, get out!"

Drake was petrified by now, looking frantically over his shoulder. He couldn't see Hornbeam anywhere. Maybe it had got lost? Or couldn't get up the slope? Either way, Drake was glad. He hurried through the three labyrinth rooms towards the rope bridge.

Again, he heard the eerie voice of the ghost Bumble: "The treasure will stay here. Leave and never return."

Drake had started walking across the bridge when he heard the large thuds of Hornbeam's footsteps. He looked down through the wooden slats of the bridge and saw a large blast of fire. It was Hornbeam. The dragon had found a way through the caves without climbing the slope and was now looking straight up at him from the deep ravine.

Drake speeded up, being careful not to slip through the slots. Hornbeam stood up on his rear legs gaining his maximum height, then breathed a giant fireball straight up towards the bridge. Drake ran, tripping and stumbling as he went.

The fire had just reached the bridge, setting alight the pieces of rope and scorching the wooden slats, making the bridge weaker.

Drake jumped the last couple of feet back to safety, when a large claw came up from the ravine, missing Drake's leg by inches; Hornbeam was crawling up to attack him. Drake looked around and saw a large rock. Picking it up, he smashed it down on the claw, breaking off one of its talons. The dragon released a gigantic roar as it fell back down to the depths below.

A relieved Drake picked up the talon like a trophy and made his way through the archway. He passed the Brunswick station, along the train track and back through the tunnel. As he ran, he heard another loud roar echoing down the tunnel. The roof collapsed and came crashing down. Large boulders smashed on to the track, blocking the tunnel. Luckily for Drake, he managed to escape it all and made it outside.

CHAPTER 6

WHERE THERE'S A WILL
THERE'S A WAY

Over the next few months, Drake halted the work on the tunnel and boarded up the entrance with signs advising, *Trespassers Keep Out*. He was left frustrated in the knowledge that a multitude of precious stones were down there but were all out of his reach.

He decided to ring one of his closest allies at the Art of Darkness: the archaeologist, Archibald Griffin. He owned a small curiosity shop selling many odd and strange items collected from his travels.

Archibald was the oldest and founding member of the club; Drake had met him many times over the years to discuss funding for archaeological digs and knew he could be approached for help. After a disagreement that had led to the cancellation of an Egyptian treasure's exhibition, Drake also knew he harboured a slight dislike towards George Bumble.

Drake confided in Archie (as he was known to his friends) how he and George had found treasure in the caves and that George had died – although he did state that George had slipped and banged his head, rather than relate the murder. He also mentioned that George had refused him possession of the treasure, and as a result, he'd released ferocious beasts from the underworld to stop him, including Hornbeam the dragon.

Archie couldn't believe what he was hearing, and was fascinated to hear about the treasure. He was saddened to hear of George's death, but also angry at him for using spells and black magic to stop a fellow member out of the club boundary. The longer Drake talked – or lied through his teeth – to Archie, including about George Bumble's ghost, the more Archie wanted to help.

"Come down to my shop tomorrow, Drake," Archie said. "I've got just the items you'll need."

The next day arrived and Drake wandered down to Archie's shop, Curiosities of the World. As he opened the door, a bell rang.

"On my way," a distant voice said. Footsteps clattered down the stairs, down the hallway and finally on to the shop floor.

"Archie, my old friend," Drake said. "How are you doing? You're looking well."

"Thank you, I feel well. Here let me take your jacket."

Archie was in his early sixties, stood at six foot two inches and was as thin as a bean pole. He had silvery grey hair which he smothered with Brylcreem for a perfect side-parting. He was always smartly dressed in a three-piece suit and smoked a tobacco pipe made of cherry wood, with a brass inlay around the stem.

His shop was a treasure trove of everything he'd collected over many years of archaeological adventures. From the vast rain forests to the temples and tombs of Egypt, Archie had a tale to tell – along with a few mementos. His biggest claim to fame (so he said), was accompanying Howard Carter to Egypt during the discovery of Tutankhamun's tomb – which he continually talked about.

Something he was less likely to talk about, was the reason he was thrown out of the Archaeological Society a few years later. On his last trip to Egypt, his team discovered the tomb of Osiris, where several items vanished. Although no real evidence ever surfaced and no artefacts were ever recovered, Archie was removed from the society for failure to keep written accounts and keep the treasure safe.

From that moment, Archie was on his own. But with his knowledge of antiquities and a newfound taste for all things mythical and paranormal, he opened his shop and started a social club for other people who shared his fascination with the strange and wonderful: the Art of Darkness.

Inside the shop were statues, puzzles, stuffed creatures and hundreds of books on everything from myths and conspiracy theories to alien landings and ghosts, all squeezed into every available space.

"Here, look at this," Archie said, handing Drake a book.

The book contained details about dragons and, more importantly, how to kill them. Sitting down in a corner, Drake read. "This is amazing," he said. "A couple of months ago I would have scoffed at what's written here, but now! Well I know exactly what I have to find."

Archie looked at him. "And that is?"

Snapping the book shut, Drake said, "Archie, I need a dragon slayer. That's the only way I'll be able to get to my treasure."

"Well, Drake, I don't think they're ten a penny around Brunswick, my old friend."

"I realise that, and maybe it's going to take a bit longer than I thought. But I will get what's mine, even if it nearly kills me."

Drake continued reading the dragon slayer myths and how these special people became slayers. The book stated that only when a newborn baby drinks the blood of a dragon on the night a blood moon travels through the constellation of Orion, is a dragon slayer created.

"Archie, have you got any books on astronomy and constellations?" Drake asked, casting his gaze over the bookcases.

"Just over here, my dear friend," Archie said, leading him around another corner. "You'll find what you need here."

Grabbing as many books as he could hold, Drake said, "I'll bring these back as soon as I can."

"Take your time," Archie said. "Good luck in finding whatever you need."

Drake read page after page about stars, galaxies and moons, trying to piece together when this phenomenon would happen again. After many hours, he calculated that the next time a blood moon would pass through the constellation of Orion would be in three years. In fact, the last time this had happened was over a century ago so there was no one around who could help him.

Drake resigned himself to the fact that he would never see the treasure again. After all, if a dragon slayer was born in three years' time, it would still be at least another twenty years before they were big and strong enough to fight a dragon.

An idea popped into his head. Instead of trying to get his own hands on the treasure he would pass on the information to his closest family: his twin grandchildren, Victor and Lance Golding. His boys, as he referred to them, were six years old. When they were grown up, they would have to deal with getting a dragon slayer down to the tunnel themselves.

That was settled, but there were other problems to be taken care of. Where was he going to get dragon's blood from? How would he get a baby to drink it? He decided to go back and see Archibald Griffin with his conundrum.

"Well, Drake," Archie said. "Unless you go back inside the tunnel and face the dragon yourself, I can't see how you can get any blood. I have a lot of stuff in this shop but dragon's blood I am sadly short of."

Drake put his hand in the pocket of his overcoat to get his wallet for the money he owed Archie. "Oh my!" he said.

"What?"

"I think I've just found what I need."

Drake pulled his hand out of the pocket, opening it up to reveal Hornbeam's claw. "Wonderful," Archie said. "Look, you can see dried blood on the broken end. Just soak it in water for a few days and hey presto, you'll have dragon's blood."

Drake took Archie's advice and extracted the blood from the claw, keeping it safe in a test tube. He knew when the next alignment with the blood moon was due and also had some dragon's blood. All he had to do now was wait.

Time passed slowly for Drake. Days seemed like weeks, and weeks felt like months. All he could think about was the birth of the chosen child.

In the town of Brunswick nobody suspected anything. The tunnel was boarded up and plans were put on hold, citing money problems as the reason. Even the disappearance of George Bumble failed to raise eyebrows. Never having been married, George had no immediate family, so Drake told people he'd travelled to Europe for business reasons. Only Drake and Archibald knew the secrets of the tunnel. That was how Drake wanted it to stay until his grandsons, Victor and Lance, could bring his plan into fruition.

After three years, the time arrived for Drake to put his plan into action. He checked with a local astrologer to make sure his calculations were correct.

They were! The blood moon was due to pass the constellation of Orion that very night. All he needed to do was to gain access to a hospital without looking suspicious.

Drake had thought about this. A couple of years earlier he'd started doing charity work at the local hospital, including contributing towards a new wing. This meant he was regularly seen walking the corridors, meeting staff and chatting with the patients.

The night came along with – just as Drake had predicted – a giant moon, the colour of blood, adorning the clear night sky, surrounded by thousands of stars, some brighter than others, both twinkling and shooting. He then saw what he'd been searching for: the constellation of Orion in all its glory. The moon was on a perfect trajectory to cross Orion's path in one hour's time. He desperately hoped a child would be born at the right hour.

When Drake arrived, he was in luck, he'd just seen a heavily pregnant woman screaming, as she was taken in from an ambulance. His plan was working perfectly. Within half an hour the screams of the woman giving birth were replaced by the noise of a baby crying. This was it; his time had come.

He waited for the midwives to take the child to clean up and then followed them. Purposefully, he bumped into them on a corner and apologised. "I'm so sorry, ladies, I didn't see you there," he said.

The nurse recognised him. "Oh, hello Mr Golding, back again are you?"

"I am, charity never ends for me. Well, look at that beautiful baby," Drake said, pointing to the newborn. "Could I?"

"Well we shouldn't, but as it's you, you can hold him while we grab some towels."

The nurses turned their backs and in an instant Drake took the small test tube of dragon's blood and poured it into the newborn's mouth. The plan had worked. The nurses returned and took the baby back to its mother.

"Have you got any names in mind?" asked the nurse.

"I've been told there's a rare star and moon alignment tonight involving the Orion constellation, so I'm going to name him Orion. But what's this?"

she asked, pointing to three tiny marks on the baby's neck.

"Don't worry," the nurse replied. "It looks like a birthmark. We'll keep an eye on it for you."

Drake made his way to the desk and got the woman's name: Beatrix Hart. Hardly containing his happiness, he made his way out of the hospital doors.

All he needed to do now was gain the mother's address; and he was sure one of his many contacts could help him with that. He would then wait, not only for the baby to grow up but for his twin grandsons also to mature.

It would be their responsibility to commence the hard work when the time came.

CHAPTER 7

A TRIP TO SCOTLAND

As the years passed, Drake nurtured his adopted twin grandchildren, Victor and Lance, through the trials and tribulations young children bring. He enjoyed the time together with them – a contrast to his own son's upbringing, due to his compulsion for work. There were even times when he'd forget all about the treasure in the tunnel, until the inevitable happened, when Drake would catch a glimpse of Beatrix Hart walking with her son, Orion, down the street. Little did Beatrix know that the man who gave a friendly smile to her and Orion, would one day organise the kidnapping of her son and leave her broken-hearted.

Victor and Lance were growing up fast. They had similar broad builds, although they weren't identical in looks. Victor had a chiselled look to him, with straight black hair; while Lance had short mousy hair with a rounded face. Once they had moved up to secondary school – Brunswick Grammar of course – Drake decided the time was right to introduce them to the Art of Darkness club. They were at that age when they were inquisitive about life and sought new experiences – this was perfect for them.

On this day, Gerald Sloane – the club chairman at the time – invited all club members to their annual excursion. This year it was a trip to Scotland, in search of the Loch Ness Monster. Victor and Lance couldn't hide their excitement.

"Please Grandad, please," Victor said. "*Please* can we go? It sounds brilliant."

"Just hang on there, young Victor. We don't just go there to find monsters. We'll be staying up late, going to the local public houses and trying their finest scotch whiskies. You're both too young."

"We'll be no trouble," said Lance. "It'll do us good to get out of Brunswick and visit somewhere new."

Drake stayed quiet for a moment, as the cogs in his head ticked over. *Maybe this could ease them into thinking that mythical creatures really do exist,* he thought.

"Listen here, boys. I'll have a talk with your nan, and if we both agree, then yes, you can come on the trip. But any messing about, you'll be severely reprimanded. Do you both understand?"

"Yes Grandad," they said in unison.

Drake and Lillian discussed the matter and, much to the boys' delight, they were allowed to go.

A few days before the trip, Drake dropped the boys off in the centre of Brunswick and gave them some money to spend on clothes. Buying warm, smart clothes was Drake's intention, but the boys had other ideas. They wanted to buy other things, things that could help them in the search for the Loch Ness Monster.

"Let's go in here," said Lance, pointing to the Army and Navy store. "They'll be loads of things in here."

"OK," Victor said. "Why don't you find a few jackets and waterproofs to keep Grandad happy, and I'll go looking for the good stuff."

Lance walked around, grabbing whatever he could find and took them to the till. "You have got to be joking!" he said, on seeing what Victor had acquired.

"What do you reckon? Nessie won't stand a chance against this." Victor stood in the aisle holding a large wooden bow, a quiver of arrows slung over his shoulder.

"Grandad is going to flip."

"Don't worry, I've always been able to charm him. Anyway, I've bought some other things as well."

Lance wandered closer to see for himself. In a basket were a pair of binoculars, a compass and a hunting knife – the size that could kill an elephant. "You do realise we're only going to Scotland to see if the Loch Ness Monster myth is true. Which part of that sentence suggests we're going on a hunting trip to shoot it with a bow and arrow, then slice it to pieces with this monstrosity of a knife?"

"It's just in case; you never know what might happen up there."

"Well as long as you take the blame, Victor."

Victor did take the blame. A bright red bruised cheek proved it. Drake didn't take fools gladly – even his own. It wasn't just the purchasing of the weapons he was angry about. He hated people going behind his back and not doing what he asked.

On the day of the trip, tensions between Drake and the boys had eased, with Drake still allowing them to join him – minus the weapons of course, which were put away in the garage. This was still a great chance for Victor and Lance to start believing in the unexplained.

After a long and bumpy, eight-hour minibus ride, they pulled up outside the bed and breakfast – home for the next two nights. It was the furthest the twins had ever travelled, which made it even more exciting for them.

Drake and the boys made their way off the bus, stretching and straightening their stiff limbs as they went. Turning around they saw their lodgings: the Urquhart View B&B. It was a beautifully renovated barn conversion, made from black and grey stone, with a dark slate roof. The boys couldn't wait to get inside and choose their beds.

"Hang on," said Drake. "Take a look at this."

The twins looked round and saw Urquhart Castle, a stone's throw from the B&B.

"Wow," Victor said. "It looks amazing."

"Can we go and explore?" asked Lance.

"I'll see if we have time tomorrow . . . I may be seeing a man about a dog." This was Drake's usual reply when going to the pub. "First we need to pack and get some dinner. We're all quite drained after that journey."

When evening arrived, Drake and the other members decided to go for a wander down the lane to the local pub, leaving Victor and Lance alone. Drake had trusted them to look after themselves, saying he'd be back by eleven at the latest. After a few hours of countless card games and boring television, the boys decided to sneak out. They headed straight for the castle – although it was more of a giant ruin than a castle. A large wall surrounded the main build, which the boys climbed and walked along.

"Look at the view, Lance. That must be Loch Ness . . . it's massive."

From the castle to the distant mountains, the

giant loch dominated the view, snaking its way through the Highlands.

"That's where the monster is then," Lance said. "I've got to be honest, I don't believe in any of that, do you?"

Victor shrugged his shoulders. "I don't know. Now we're here, it does have that mystical feel about it."

"I'm glad yee said that," said a voice out of nowhere.

The twins looked at each other in silence, gesturing with their hands to where the voice had come from.

"I'm doon here," the voice said in a strong Scottish accent.

Looking down below at the other side of the wall they saw an old man sitting on a log. "What should we do?" Lance whispered.

"He looks normal enough," Victor replied. "Anyway, there's two of us if he tries anything."

The boys jumped down to introduce themselves. "Hi, I'm Victor and this is Lance. You gave us quite a fright there. Who are you?"

"My name's Dougal MacDonald. I'm the caretaker

here. Shouldn't you wee laddies be inside at this time of neet?"

Victor looked confused. He'd never met someone with a strong regional English dialect before, never mind a Scottish one as strong as Dougal's. "Can you talk a bit slower please, I . . ."

"Sorry, Dougal," Lance butted in. "What my brother is trying to say is that we're not from these parts. We just came to explore this castle, but we'll be on our way now."

"You're the wee laddie who doesna believe in Nessie then?"

"I suppose so. It just seems impossible for a dinosaur type of creature to be living in these waters."

"Just because it happened in times gone by, doesna mean it's not here now. What happens if the hands of the clocks stop turning . . . time is extinguished? It's timeless here. Look at the mountains and the loch. They've not changed for a million years; time has passed 'em by. Dinnae let your doubts take over your imagination. When you're standing looking at the loch tomorrow, you'll get a sensation that something is there with you . . . that something is watching you. There's a reason for that."

"Victor! Lance!" a voice echoed through the valley.

"It's Grandad," Lance said. "He's looking for us. He's back early."

Victor took control of the situation and popped his head over the wall. "Oh, hi Grandad," he said as Drake stood over him. "I hope you didn't mind me and Lance having a little exploration of the castle ruins?"

Drake wasn't the calmest of people sober, never mind after several whiskies. He grabbed Victor by his collar and lifted him up to his side of the wall. Lance stood and quickly followed suit.

"When I say stay in your room, I mean it! Can't you see how bad this looks on me in front of my esteemed friends? Especially as I had to ask permission from the club to bring you both. Anything could have happened to you out here. You don't know who's wandering about."

Lance put his hand up to speak. "We're fine, Grandad; we met a local man who told us about Nessie."

"And . . . where is he?"

"He's just below this . . ." Lance fell silent as he looked over the wall, to find nobody there. "Well, er, he must have walked off. But he was there!"

Drake grabbed both boys by the arms and marched them back to the B&B.

The next morning at breakfast, Victor and Lance were still trying to convince Drake that they had met Dougal.

"I'm sorry laddies, I couldn't help but overhear you talking about someone called Dougal," said the landlady, putting an extra plate of toast on their table.

"You see, Grandad, we weren't lying," said Victor, giving his brother a sly wink.

"He often comes here to see us," she said.

"He seemed a really nice man, from what we could understand from him," Victor continued. "He was trying to convince Lance that the monster really does exist."

The lady looked down on Lance, "You're not a believer, wee lad?"

"Not . . . really," he said, trying not to hurt the woman's feelings.

The lady burst out laughing.

"What's so funny?"

"It's funny how you don't believe in Nessie, but you believe in ghosts."

"What do you mean?" a puzzled Lance said.

"Dougal MacDonald died twenty years ago. You were talking to a ghost!"

The boys dropped their cutlery in shock, staring at each other, speechless.

Drake clapped his hands, "Well, well. This is a turn up for the books," he said. "I brought you up here to broaden your horizons and it turns out you've both seen a ghost at first hand. Who needs the Loch Ness Monster?"

Victor and Lance spent the rest of their breakfast in silence. They couldn't believe what they'd been told.

In the next couple of days, Drake and the boys searched and searched for Nessie, but to no avail. Not a single sighting of any monster, giant eel, Plesiosaurus, even Dougal – or any other ghost come to think of it – were spotted. Drake was happy though. He knew that even without Nessie, the boys realised there were things out there that couldn't be explained.

CHAPTER 8

DRAKE'S LONG WAIT

Sixteen years later, Drake Golding was an elderly man in his late seventies, while Victor and Lance had reached their late twenties and had grown up to be clever and determined young men. Drake was immensely proud.

Both men were married, and Victor had a little boy. But it was Beatrix Hart's boy, Orion, that Drake had been thinking about more than anyone. Throughout the last twenty years Drake had made sure he knew where Orion and his mum were. He knew where they lived, which schools he went to, which clubs he attended and even which girlfriend he had.

Orion married Melanie at eighteen, a girl he had met at school. They had one son called Leo, now a year old. Orion worked at the local steelworks when he left school, but unfortunately the company went bust, leaving Orion doing odd jobs to pay the bills. Melanie worked part time as a nanny to help with the income and despite their financial problems, they still remained happily in love.

The time had come for Drake to sit down with Victor and Lance and tell them the story of the Brunswick Tunnel. He had no doubts that they would listen to him, especially after the Loch Ness trip and others they had taken since with the Art of Darkness. They had seen many things that others simply did not believe in. The brothers sat opposite him and took in every word Drake said. Their eyes lit up when he told them about the treasure and diamonds.

"This is crazy," Lance said.

Drake nodded, "I know, and you won't believe it till you actually get there and see it for yourself."

"And you're sure this Orion guy is a slayer?" Victor asked.

"I can't be 100 per cent," Drake replied. "It's

impossible to know until he comes near a dragon. Even he doesn't know he's a slayer yet. But I do know something; just like any parent, he'd do anything you told him to do if he knew his family were in danger."

"You mentioned a ghost as well?" Lance said.

"Ha, you read my mind, young Lance," Drake said as he pulled his chair nearer to them. "An old friend dropped this off at my house a few years ago." Drake reached over and picked a small box off the side table. "I have Archibald Griffin to thank for this . . . do you remember him? He was having a clear out of his shop as he was retiring and came across it. Remembering my story, he thought it would come in handy one day. Unfortunately, Archie died a few months later."

"So, what is it?" Victor asked.

"It's a prison . . . a prison for ghosts," Drake replied as he passed it to the boys.

"What are these marks on the side for?" Victor asked.

"They're hieroglyphics; what the ancient Egyptians used to communicate with," Drake replied. "Archie told me he got it from Egypt a long time ago.

He said you open it up and translate the symbols under the lid. This captures a ghost, until someone reads aloud the external symbols. The ghost will then be set free."

"And it's as easy as that?" Lance laughed.

"Apparently so, that's what Archie told me, and I trusted him," Drake replied. "Oh, and before I forget, you'll need a few of these."

Drake handed over a few sticks of dynamite to his grandsons. "When I was leaving the tunnel, part of the roof collapsed. I haven't been back since, so just in case it's blocked, these will help you."

Victor and Lance both stood up and thanked their grandad. "We won't let you down," Lance vowed. "We'll get back what is rightfully ours."

The brothers decided to follow Orion around for a few weeks and get used to his schedule. They noticed that every Saturday, he would go fishing to the lake in the nearby forest. This was perfect, a place with no one else around and not too far away from the tunnel entrance.

They packed a few bits and bobs to take with them including rope, torches, knives and the dynamite.

Victor also had his old bow with a quiver of arrows with him, which he'd found lying around in his garage – causing him a wry smile at his youthful antics.

Lance brought a gift his grandad had given him: a handgun. They also had something to send Orion to sleep with. During another hospital charity function, Drake had stolen a bottle of chloroform from the hospital. This went slightly awry when he was caught on camera by a trainee nurse, thus creating a few court dates and a slap on the wrist. That hadn't been beneficial to his standing in the town, nor his health for that matter.

Saturday arrived with the sun shining bright over the town of Brunswick. Victor and Lance made their way through the gardens, peppered with blossom trees, and towards the forest. Victor decided to take a fishing rod as well just to avoid suspicion, and it meant they could get closer to Orion without him noticing anything odd. The men arrived at a large gate and climbed over it.

"You know, this day is going to change our lives forever," Lance said.

"Yeah, just think we'll never have to work again if what Grandad says about the treasure is true," Victor replied.

Lance stopped walking, "You think Grandad was telling lies?"

"No, not as such, but he might be exaggerating in his old age. However, we do owe it to him to see this through; he wouldn't put us in too much danger."

They wove through the trees until in the distance they could see water flickering between the branches. Victor grabbed Lance's arm. "OK this is it," he whispered. "We'll walk slowly up to him, and if he notices us, just act cool and talk fishing."

Victor and Lance watched Orion lying down in his usual spot. He was by the large tree roots with his fishing rod in the water, next to a large holding net. Luckily for the twins, Orion was having a nap.

As they approached, they tried to avoid standing on twigs which could alert their target. Lance pulled out a handkerchief soaked in chloroform and attacked him, grabbing his head and forcing the hanky over his face. Orion kicked and flailed his arms, but Victor grabbed hold of them, and tied his wrists behind him. Gradually, the movements of Orion reduced as the chloroform subdued his body. Then there was nothing; Orion was out for the count.

Victor had a good look around in case anyone had seen the struggle. "Think we're fine, Lance," he said. "Now, let's get a move on. First let's get his fishing stuff packed away; we can't afford to leave any traces."

Both men scrambled Orion's possessions together, packing them away in a rucksack. Lance grabbed the fishing equipment and rucksack while Victor, the stronger of the two, put Orion over his shoulder and headed off towards the embankment. "Are you OK carrying him, Victor?" Lance asked, pacing ahead.

"Should be fine, don't think it's too far to the tunnel entrance from here."

Making their way along the embankment, they pushed and fought through the bramble bushes, dodging the low branches until they saw the descent. They climbed down and continued walking until they reached the boarded-up tunnel. "Wow he's heavy . . .

I need to catch my breath," Victor said.

"Not here you don't," Lance remarked. "Let's get inside first. Another few hours and people will be out searching for him."

Lance pulled the boarding back, allowing Victor to pull Orion inside. Once everything else was in, he closed it again. Turning on his torch, he shone it down the tunnel. "I hope you're feeling strong," Lance said. "This could take a while."

"Think we'll take it in turns," Victor said, with a raised eyebrow. "So, anyway, this is the famous tunnel, is it? Don't seem to be many dragons lurking down here."

"Ha-ha, hopefully you're right, Brother, although Grandad did say a part of the ceiling had collapsed forming a barrier, which I presume would also stop anything bad getting out."

The two brothers carried on down the track, taking it in turns to carry Orion. Eventually they came to the wall of boulders. "Grandad was right about needing the dynamite," Lance said, shining his torch. "It's blocked from the floor to the roof."

"I'll climb up first," Victor said. "There may be a gap higher up."

Laying Orion down on the wet floor, Victor leapt up on to the boulders. "Any luck?" Lance shouted up.

"No, we'll have to use the dynamite." Victor jumped down and pulled four sticks from his rucksack. "How many will we need?"

"Just the one, I think," Lance replied. "Any more and we'll do too much damage. We may also need the rest for what lies ahead."

"That's a good point," Victor said, lodging one of the sticks into the base of the boulders.

Making sure Lance had dragged Orion far enough back from the wall, Victor lit the dynamite then ran back to join his brother.

BOOM! The tunnel filled up with smoke, spraying rock fragments that nearly hit the three men. "Well, there's nothing like making a quiet entrance, and that wasn't it," Lance remarked. "Every dragon and creature in the world will know we're on the way now!"

"Stop worrying, look! It's made a hole big enough for us to get through."

The boys pulled Orion through the gap, making their way to the other side. "Wow, this is special,"

Lance said, looking around. "It looks brand new. We must be close to the station."

"What are they?" Victor asked, pointing to the roof.

"They look like giant glow worms. Turn off your torch."

After switching off their torches, the tunnel remained ablaze with light. "Are these some of the creatures Grandad was telling us about?" Victor asked.

"I presume so, though they don't seem that scary, they're more of a help than a hindrance."

The fishing gear had become a burden, so Lance dumped it against the tunnel wall. "Oh you poor thing!" Victor shouted. "Shame I can't do that with Orion."

"There's no point in bringing it with us any further is there?" Lance replied. "No one's going to find it up here!"

As they continued on down the track, they saw the station ahead. Receiving a much-needed moral boost, their steps increased, and Orion's weight seemed to lessen. "Brunswick Station!" Lance announced on reading the sign. "At last we've arrived."

"Thank goodness for that," Victor said, laying Orion down on the platform. "This is pretty impressive; the detail is amazing. It would have made an excellent attraction."

"I know," Lance said, looking inside the waiting room. "And just think our grandfather owns all this."

At those words a large gust of wind blew up the tunnel, nearly knocking Victor over. The howling wind grew stronger and stronger, spinning in a circle until it created a dust cloud. Turning away to protect their eyes, both men jumped into the waiting room. From inside they noticed the wind subsiding, leaving a ghostly figure floating over the track. The apparition moved towards the waiting room where the brothers stood in shock. "You two cowards, come to me!" the ghost demanded in a deep, thunderous voice.

Lance glanced at Victor. "Grandad was telling the truth . . . wasn't he?"

"It looks like it," Victor replied. "This must be the ghost of George Bumble."

Both men stepped out of the waiting room and on to the platform. "Do you know who I am?" asked the ghost.

"You're George Bumble," Victor replied. "Or at least what's left of him."

The ghost floated higher, "So you two must be Drake's grandsons, Victor and Lance. Come for the treasures, have we? Greed must run through Golding blood."

"We've come for our family's treasure, and there's nothing you can do to stop us," Victor said, defiantly.

A strange noise emanated from the end of the platform. Orion was slowly coming around and regaining consciousness. Bumble's ghost floated over to him and spoke, "And who have you brought with you?"

"Not that it's any of your business but we've covered all eventualities, including killing the dragon that's supposedly guarding our treasure," Lance said.

"He's a dragon slayer?" Bumble's ghost enquired.

"Correct, and we've got a little something for you as well," Lance said, taking out the small cube from his rucksack. "You know, Bumble, all this would have been so unnecessary if you'd only given our grandad the treasure instead of being so high and mighty about it all."

Pulling the lid off the box, Lance turned towards the ghostly figure of George Bumble. Before the ghost had time to realise what was happening, he read out the phrase that he'd previously deciphered: "THIS WILL HOLD THE SPIRIT SAFE, AWAY FROM THE ENTIRE HUMAN RACE."

A large beam of light shot out from the box, covering Bumble's ghostly presence. Lance held tight, while Victor and a very dazed Orion looked on. Within an instant the beam had absorbed George Bumble's spirit into the box. Slamming shut the lid, Lance put it down next to him and shouted, "It's worked!"

Victor stood up, "It's all true. But that means the rest of the stories are true as well."

"What's true?" Orion said shakily, as the chloroform wore off. "I heard that ghost thing say your names are Lance and Victor. You know you won't get away with this, so tell me what the heck is going on!"

The two brothers walked over to Orion, grabbing his arms and lifting him to his feet. "You'll find out soon enough," Victor said, taping his mouth shut. "Oh, and Lance, don't forget the box."

"Don't worry, I'm going to put it somewhere safe, there's no point taking it through all the tunnels with us." Lance picked up the box from the platform and placed it in the water tank next to the signal box. "I'll grab it on our way out."

They both walked Orion further along the track until they came to an opening and the large archway inscribed with the word *Labyrinth*.

"Grandad told us to walk through here to get to the bridge," Lance said.

"I'll put my torch on," Victor said. "These glow worm creatures are too high up now. We need to find the bridge."

They walked through the archway with Victor shining his torch.

"Is that it?" Lance said, looking at a very burnt and rickety bridge.

"I guess so. Not sure we should all cross it at the same time, though."

Victor shone his torch over the edge of the chasm, searching for the bottom, but there was nothing. A few bats flew up, slicing through the torch beam. "You know if this bridge breaks that's the end of us. No one could survive falling from this height," he said.

Pushing Orion forward, Lance said, "Let him go first. If the bridge falls at least we survive."

"Good idea," Victor replied, tearing the tape off Orion's mouth. "Right, you don't know us, and you don't want to know us, but do as we say and you and your family will be fine."

"What? You leave my family alone. I mean it," Orion pleaded. "What did that ghostly voice say about a dragon slayer?"

Victor stood close to Orion face to face. "Listen," he said. "We believe you're a dragon slayer and we need you to do a very important job for us."

Orion laughed, "A what? A dragon slayer? I don't even know what one of them is, never mind be one. I'm not helping you fools; you've obviously got the wrong person."

Victor grabbed his jaw, "You will do what we say,

or we'll kill your little boy, Leo. Do you understand those words, FOOL?"

"How do you know about Leo?" Orion asked.

"We know everything about you, right from the day you were born to this very moment," Lance said, taking out his gun and pointing it at Orion. "Now walk across this bridge and try to be careful. Oh, and nothing silly, remember your family."

The brothers watched as Orion tentatively made his way on to the damaged, creaking bridge. It wasn't made any easier by the fact his hands were still tied behind his back. "When you reach the other side, don't do anything stupid," Lance warned.

"Don't worry, my family is too important. I'll do what you say," Orion said, looking back at the looming gun.

Orion stepped on to the wooden slats which creaked ominously under his weight. The ropes were burnt and frayed, straining as he moved into the middle of the bridge.

"Keep going, you'll soon be there," Lance encouraged.

"It's going to break; I can feel it!" Orion yelled.

"Well, you better hurry up then," Victor shouted back.

Orion progressed as quickly as possible in the poor light, until with relief, he stepped off the bridge. "I've made it!" he shouted back.

"Right, wait there," Victor said. "I'm coming over."

Making his way over to a boulder with the intention of having a rest, Orion felt very strange. It was as if a surge of power and strength was running through every vein of his body.

Victor, who was still crossing the bridge, hadn't noticed anything, so Orion forced apart his tied hands, breaking the rope with ease. He couldn't believe it. He was so strong, but why? Quickly putting his arms back behind him, pretending he was still tied up, he watched as Victor reached his side of the chasm. "OK, it's not too bad. You can come over now," Victor advised his brother.

Lance walked on to the bridge as Victor approached Orion. "Now remember to do exactly what we say, your family's lives are at stake," Victor said, taking out his bow and arrow and pointing it at Orion.

Staring back, Orion asked, "But how can I trust you? My family may already be dead."

"Well they might, Orion, well they might," came the laughing retort.

On hearing this laugh, Orion couldn't contain his anger anymore. He brought his freed arms around, knocking the bow and arrow out of Victor's hand with such force that they flew backwards, over the edge of the ravine. He grabbed Victor by the neck; his strength was overpowering, and he easily lifted Victor high against the cave wall.

"Help! Put me down," Victor said, his face getting redder and redder.

"No. You've asked for this. You kidnapped me, hurt my family and for what? A favour for your grandad's greed."

During all this, Lance had made it halfway across the bridge, unsure whether to carry on or head back. He could only hear voices in the dim light of the cave. "Are you all right?" Lance shouted. "I'll be with you in a minute."

"No! Get back!" Victor screamed. "Orion's freed himself."

"I've got my gun; I'll shoot him."

"No, you can't see . . . it's too dark, you might shoot me. Save yourself . . . run!"

Orion turned around, still gripping Victor, and made his way back to the bridge. He was feeling and getting stronger by the minute. His veins pulsed through his forearms as if they were straining to be free.

He reached the edge of the ravine and lifted Victor high above his head then, with the ease of a child throwing a ball, he threw Victor at the bridge. The already damaged ropes of the bridge snapped, causing some of the wooden slats to split and fall apart.

Victor fell through the bridge, releasing a harrowing scream as he plummeted downwards.

The rocks under Orion's feet started to give way, making him lose his footing. He tried to grab one of the bridge anchors but to no avail. With a large echoing cry for help, Orion followed Victor to the bottom of the precipice.

Meanwhile Lance, who was running back over the bridge when it collapsed, had managed to cling to one of the wooden slats as it bashed against the side of the ravine. Climbing one rung at a time he made it back to safety.

In complete shock at what had just happened, his first thought was to see if he could climb down to check his brother was still alive. But there was no path down, just a sheer drop.

He shone his torch downwards, but the light didn't reach the bottom. Deep down he knew Victor couldn't have survived the fall. But what about Orion? Did he survive the fall? Would he come back and try to kill him? And what about the treasure waiting to be found?

Lance decided he had to get out of the tunnel as fast as possible. He picked himself up and ran down the railway line. When he arrived at the boulders halfway down the tunnel, he squeezed through the gap. Once through, he found another stick of dynamite, placed it in the hole and lit it. With a loud boom the rocks fell down and covered the small gap, blocking the tunnel once again – more importantly, not letting anything or anyone out.

Lance continued on his way out of the tunnel

thinking about what to tell Victor's wife, child and of course his Grandad Drake. But one thing was for sure, he wanted revenge and to get his hands on the treasure. Just like Drake had before him.

CHAPTER 9

1990

THE GHOST OF BUMBLE

A ghostly figure appeared from the cube.

"I want my mum," Leo muttered, clinging on to Marshall and Olly's hands for dear life.

"What . . . er . . . who are you?" Olly asked, with his bottom lip trembling.

"Well, first of all, I would like to say thank you," said the ghost.

"Enough's enough, come on guys," Leo said, shaking. "Let's get out of here, I'm scared."

The three boys shuffled their feet backwards, each one as frightened as the next.

"No! Don't go, please stay," said the ghost in a calm, friendly voice. Moving away from the cube, the ghost floated silently towards them. It appeared to be dressed in a suit with an old and round face, white hair and a large, matching bushy beard.

The boys stopped moving as the apparition neared. "What do we do?" Leo whispered.

"Not sure," Marshall said. "But by the look of him I think we're safe, he just looks like an old man."

"Come here and sit down," the ghost said, pointing to the platform.

The three boys made their tentative way to the edge of the platform, sat down and listened.

"My name is . . . I mean my name was, Mr George Bumble. I've been trapped in this prison for many years. Until you released me."

"What happened to you?" Olly asked.

George Bumble's ghost explained the story about his and Drake Golding's ambitious plans for the tunnel and their subsequent disagreement leading to his death. He also outlined how he had summoned creatures of the underworld to guard the treasure, including Hornbeam, the dragon.

"So how did you end up in the cube?" Marshall asked.

"Never mind that," Olly said. "You're saying there are things down here that could kill us?"

"Possibly, I don't know. I was locked away for a long time," the ghost said. "And to answer your first question, well, Drake's family did it; two of them with another person they'd kidnapped to help them. They opened up the cube, translated the message and imprisoned me before I had chance to react."

"Who was the other person, please? What did he look like?" a hopeful Leo asked.

"It's hard to remember, but he looked quite tall with blond hair," the ghost replied. "The men had brought him along to get the treasure."

"It must be him!" Leo shouted. "It's my dad."

"Calm down," Marshall said. "Remember this was a long time ago, anything could have happened to him by now."

"Including still being alive!" Olly said. "But how could he have helped them?"

"They said he was a dragon slayer," the ghost replied.

"A what? A dragon slayer?" Leo asked.

The ghostly spirit nodded its head, "Yes, they needed someone to kill the dragon that guards the treasure. For some reason, he was the person they chose."

"Did they kill it?" Marshall asked.

"I don't know. Like I said, they trapped me in this cube, leaving my spirit to rot. But now I've been set free and I've told you everything. It's my time for the heavens above to come and collect me; take me somewhere safe, away from this tunnel that's kept me prisoner for all these years."

A light appeared above the ghost and widened as it approached his spirit. Looking at the children one last time, he blew them a kiss and whispered, "Thank you." On the trail of his words, his spirit floated up to the light and disappeared. The light closed behind him.

"Whoa!" Leo said. "That was amazing."

Olly agreed. "It sure was, and we know your dad was here and why they brought him here. Although how the heck is he a dragon slayer?"

"Come on, then, let's find them all," Marshall said.

"Hang on, Marshall. We don't know if they killed anything. Are they still here or did they leave the caves empty handed?" Olly replied.

"I'm not sure. I just know I've got a feeling that someone's still in here."

Leo stood up, "Me too, I think my dad's here, and I think he's still alive."

"Well OK, we're a team so let's carry on looking," said Olly.

Jumping off the platform, the boys headed down the track with a spring in their steps. In front of them was the large archway with the word *LABYRINTH* engraved into it. "Remember what the ghost told us," Leo said. "Through the archway we'll find a bridge leading to a set of labyrinth-type caves."

"OK, race you!" Marshall said.

They took off in a sprint, running to reach the bridge first. "Stop!" Olly shouted. "Stop!"

The three boys skidded to a halt, kicking a few stones which rolled and fell down the steep ravine.

"Blimey, where's the bridge gone?" Leo gasped.

Marshall knelt down and grabbed something hanging down the cliff. "Look, part of it's still here. It must have broken."

Olly shone his torch over the ravine, "Yeah, you can see it hanging down the other side as well."

Leo was dejected. "But if there's no bridge, I can't find my dad."

"Don't give up hope just yet," Olly said, as positive as ever. "Let's all have a look in our rucksacks and see what we've got to help us."

As they were looking, Leo heard a rustling noise above them. Pointing his torch upwards he released an anguished scream. "Aaaarrgghh!"

"What?" Marshall said, falling backwards on to his bum.

"Look at that," Leo said, shaking his torch.

Perched up high on the ceiling was a giant spider. No, not a giant spider; an enormous eight-legged monster, the size of a car.

Olly grabbed the others, pulling them away. "Keep shining your torch on it, Leo," he said. "Don't let it out of your sight."

"Don't worry I won't. But what are we going to do?"

"Hang on," Marshall said, rummaging through his bag. "Use this!"

From out of the rucksack he produced a ten-inch knife. "What did you bring that for?" Olly said, shocked.

"For circumstances like this!"

"Well I'm not going to kill it. I've never killed anything in my life."

"Hey lads!" Leo whispered. "It's coming down towards us on its silk. Hurry up and think of something."

Marshall grabbed the knife back. "If you want a job doing, do it yourself." He lifted up his arm and threw the knife at the spider. It shimmered as it spun through the air like a Catherine wheel until it struck the spider, piercing its body. It was killed instantly.

"Where did you learn to do that?" Leo asked.

"My uncle, he takes me hunting in the countryside."

Olly walked up to the dead spider. "Look at this lads. Its silk is still attached."

"So, what do you want us to do . . . make a web?" Marshall asked, each word dripping sarcasm.

"No, you idiot. Don't you see? It's our way of getting over the ravine. Spider's silk is one of the strongest materials known to man and with the size of this spider, the silk should easily be able to carry our weight."

Marshall wandered over, pulled the knife out of the spider's body, and cut through the silk, leaving a thick tendril dangling from the ceiling.

"Cheers, mate," Olly said. "Now, who wants to try it out first?"

Leo raised his arm, as if in a classroom, "I'll have a go. It's my dad we're trying to find, so let me risk my life first." Grabbing the silk, he pulled his body up, wrapping his legs around tight. "Seems all right to me," he said bouncing up and down like he was riding a pogo stick.

"Right, Leo," Olly said, as he and Marshall placed their arms on Leo's back. "We're going to push you off the edge and let you swing over. When you've landed, tie your rucksack to the silk and push it back over to us. You sure you're OK with this?"

"Not really but there's no choice, my dad could be over there."

"OK," Olly said. "On the count of three we're going to push you. One . . . two . . . three."

"Wooohooo!" Leo screamed as he swung across like a giant pendulum. He landed with a thud.

"Leo!" Marshall shouted. "Are you all right? Did you make it?"

"I'm fine, I'm over. It worked!" he said, tying the silk to his bag.

Marshall grabbed the bag as it appeared through the darkness, said a quick prayer and swung over, hastily followed by Olly.

"So, what's the plan now?" Marshall asked.

"The plan is to find his dad and to get the hell out of here. Although by what George Bumble's ghost implied, I've got a feeling it isn't going to be plain sailing," Olly replied.

The three boys brushed themselves down and made their way towards the first of the labyrinth caves. "Mr Bumble was right, here are the caves," Leo said. "I just hope we can get through them safely."

"We'll be fine," Marshall said. "Three brains are better than one."

Olly laughed. "Yes, but we've only got two."

"And what do you mean by that?"

"Only joking mate, only joking."

At the entrance was the riddle which read:

IN THE MAZE, YOU MUST GO.
THE CLOCK IS TICKING, DON'T BE SLOW.

Composing themselves, the boys stepped through the entrance. The maze was full of dusty glass and mirrors. "Now stay close," Olly said.

The torches were switched on, lighting up the whole room, reflecting the beams off every angle. "Actually, this could be quite fun," Leo quipped. "I love puzzles."

Olly looked at him. "It may look fun, but remember what the ghost told us about him filling the caves with demons of the underworld. There could be something around every corner."

Leo's smile vanished as he clung on to Olly for dear life.

"Right lads, steady as we go," Marshall said, leading the way.

The walls or mirrors and glass made it extremely confusing. They took it in turns walking straight into a glass pane and bashing their noses. "How big is this maze?" Leo asked.

"Don't know, it's hard to tell," Marshall replied, stretching his arms in an effort to avoid any more bumps.

"What's that?" Leo exclaimed.

"What's what?" Olly replied.

"I'm sure I just saw something looking at me from over there."

Marshall looked around and laughed. "You've probably seen your own reflection. You are quite scary."

"Very funny," Leo replied. "But I know what I saw."

Marshall turned around, still trying to find the exit to the maze. "Aaaarrgghh!"

"Now what?" said Olly.

"Leo's right," Marshall said, trembling. "There's something in here, I've just seen it . . . it was looking straight at me."

"What is it, then?"

"I don't know, but it was behind that glass panel a second ago," Marshall said, pointing his shaking finger.

"What did it look like?"

"It had red eyes, but the rest of its body was kind of moving, like a liquid."

"Right!" Olly said. "Let's speed up in here; things are getting weird. There must be a way out somewhere."

All three boys started to jog around, urgently trying to find a way out.

"Oh my God!" Olly said. "I've just seen one now, they're trying to get to us."

A splashing noise echoed around the maze – the result of the creatures throwing themselves at the glass and mirrors. Harder and harder they hit the glass until cracks appeared, allowing their liquid to seep through.

"Look! This way," Marshall said, finding an opening.

The boys ran for their lives towards the exit as more panes of glass cracked then shattered behind them. "Here, help me with this," Olly shouted to Marshall on seeing a large door. "This will keep them at bay for a while."

They slammed the door shut and all the boys breathed a huge sigh of relief. "What were they?" Leo asked.

"No idea," Olly replied puffing his cheeks. "But one thing's for sure, they're not from this world."

The boys stepped into the adjoining cave. Above the entrance was another phrase which Marshall announced by torchlight:

DON'T LOOK DOWN, THE PATH IS CLEAR.
WILL YOUR NERVES CONTROL THE FEAR?

"I hope it's nothing too high up," Leo said. "I hate heights."

"I think heights are the least of our problems," Olly said, pointing his torch beam into the cave.

Marshall and Leo popped their heads through the opening to see a narrow walkway, barely wide enough to put both feet together. At either side was not a body of water as before, but a river of bubbling lava. Giant bats glided from one end to the other.

"Blimey, my legs are shaking already." Leo squirmed. "How are we going to do this?"

Marshall walked forward. "Very slowly, and keep your eyes focused ahead. Just one foot at a time and forget about the bats, they'll be more scared of us."

The cave was stifling hot from the lava flow and

129

the ceiling dripped with condensation, making the walkway treacherous. Marshall led the way while Olly took up the rear position, keeping a watchful eye on the young Leo. "Well done!" Olly shouted over the noise of the bubbling lava.

"Cheers, but I'm starting to feel a little lightheaded with all this heat."

"We'll grab a drink when we get through this cave," Marshall replied, closing in on the other side.

"OK," Leo said. "That would be . . . Aaaarrgghh!"

Marshall looked around and saw Leo slipping off the edge of the walkway. "Noooooo!" Olly shouted, as he watched helplessly.

Just as Leo was about to fall into the boiling hot lava, a giant bat stuck its talons into his shoulders and lifted him above the path. The others tried reaching up to grab one of Leo's legs, but to no avail.

"Help me!" Leo shouted as the bat flew higher towards the ceiling and through an opening into another cave.

"Quick, Olly, get to the other side," Marshall said.

"I'm getting there. It's very slippy."

Both boys reached the end of the walkway feeling

mentally drained at this latest turn of events. "Well, this is just great. What are we meant to do now? We set out to find Leo's father and now we've lost Leo as well," Olly moaned.

"And we'll continue on to find his father. We know we're on the right track."

"But what about Leo? Where's he gone? Is he still alive?"

"I'm sure he is, I can feel it in my bones," Marshall said, putting a comforting arm around Olly. "He's a clever lad . . . he'll probably find his dad before we do."

"Not sure how much more of this I can take. How many more of these caves are there?"

"Think there's just one more. That's what the ghost told us anyway and after that, well, who knows what lies ahead?"

They reached the next and final labyrinth cave. Once again Olly read the phrase out above the opening:

PLEASE BE QUICK ACROSS THIS WEB,
DON'T WAKE THE SPIDER, IT'S NOT BEEN FED.

"Well this doesn't bode well if you don't like spiders," Marshall said.

As they looked through the entrance, they saw a massive spider's web spanning the whole length of the cave. Underneath, there was more lava flow bubbling away furiously. "You just have to crawl over this web to get to the other side. Maybe it's not so bad after all," Olly said.

"You might want to look over there," Marshall whispered, pointing his torch into the corner of the cave.

"I hope that's not what I think it is," Olly said, unable to blink.

"Well, if you think it's another giant spider bigger than a dog, you'd be right," Marshall said. "It looks asleep at the moment so let's not make any sudden movement while we cross the web."

Olly grabbed his arm, "Cross the web! Are you mental? I'm not going anywhere near that thing."

"We have no choice. It's the only way forward. Leo's father is in here and so is Leo, we owe it to them both to keep going,"

"We're going to risk our lives for someone who might not even be alive?"

"Yes!" Marshall replied. "It's what we set out to do, to find Leo's dad, dead or alive. And who knows what else is waiting for us in the caves."

"What do you mean, what else?" Olly asked.

"I don't know, but let's face it, since we've entered this tunnel, we've found a long-lost train station, a ghost, giant bats and creatures that seem to be made out of water."

"OK, I get your point. But it doesn't really make me want to go further in, hearing about all these things."

"What I'm trying to say is, there are things that we could never imagine seeing so there might be good things that happen to us as well, like finding Leo and his dad. But we'll never know if we don't carry on."

Olly took a deep breath and puffed his cheeks, releasing a big sigh. "Right, OK. But I'm doing this purely for Leo and his dad," he said. "Not for your excitement."

"That's fine, you won't regret it," Marshall said, smiling.

The boys got down on to their hands and knees and climbed on to the web. "Wasn't this originally meant to have been made of rope?" Olly asked.

"Probably," Marshall whispered. "But I think the spider's been adding its own silk to it since the caves were overrun with the afterlife."

"Great! As if this wasn't hard enough to start with."

Carefully, they made their way to the middle of the web, making sure not to wake the giant spider. They could see the exit door in the distance through the steam rising from the bubbling lava below them. Unbeknown to them, however, a small knife had pierced through the bottom of Olly's rucksack, sometimes catching parts of the web as he crawled along, "We're nearly there, Marshall, just another twenty yards."

"OK, keep concentrating, mate."

They continued along when Olly slowed. "What's wrong?" Marshall asked.

"It's fine. My rucksack keeps getting stuck. I'll give it a quick tug."

The knife sliced through one of the spider's silks making it spring back like an enormous elastic band. Falling under the web, Olly grabbed hold of another strand of silk as he held on for dear life.

"Olly! Hold on! I'll come and get you."

Just as Marshall made his way back, he felt intense vibrations emanating from the web. Looking across to the side he realised the giant spider had awoken and was scuttling towards them. "The spider, Olly!" Marshall shouted again. "It's coming for you."

"Aaaarrgghh!" Olly screamed as the eight-legged beast pounded over. "I can't move, I'm all tangled in its silk."

Marshall panicked. "I don't know what to do. I've got the knife, but I can't get a clear shot for all this webbing."

"Just throw the damn thing."

Grabbing the knife, Marshall launched it towards the spider. Unfortunately, the wrong end hit the spider's head, and the knife bounced off, falling into the lava below.

The spider reared up on its back legs and, with sheer anger blazing in its eyes, opened its mouth, displaying two talon-like fangs. It dwarfed poor Olly, who was holding on by his fingertips to the silk.

"Well this is it, Marshall . . . I'm going to die," Olly

accepted, as the spider reached down to him.

"No. You're not!" a voice bellowed from high up in the cave. In the next moment, a flaming arrow with the intensity of a lightning bolt flew through the air. The cave was instantly illuminated.

The arrow shot straight into the spider's abdomen, knocking it backwards on to the web. Another arrow quickly followed, disabling the creature.

Olly managed to get his leg free and kicked the spider, sending it falling with a sickening screech into the hot lava.

Marshall hurried along the web to help Olly up. "What and who was that?"

"Not sure," Olly said, shaking. "But whatever it was just saved my life."

Making their way off the web on to the cave floor, Marshall shouted out. "Hello, who are you?"

His words echoed around the tunnels as Olly caught his breath and realised. "You know who it could be, don't you?" he said.

"You think it's Orion."

"Well, who else could it be? Let me shout this

time." Olly took a deep breath and boomed. "Is that you, Orion, if so, we're here to help. We've come with your son."

"Leo?" the voice echoed back.

Olly looked around, trying to see who it was that had spoken. "Yes, yes. We've come to rescue you."

The boys fell silent for a few seconds, when they heard something scurrying around high up in the cave. Fragments of rock fell to the ground. Finding his torch, Olly shone it on to the walls. All of a sudden, a large thud sounded behind them. They spun around.

In front of them stood a tall man clutching a bow. He had dirty, long hair with a matching beard. His clothes were torn and stained, but he looked healthy. With muscles like a Roman gladiator, he also carried a quiver of arrows draped over his shoulder.

"You're Orion, aren't you?" Olly asked.

"I am," Orion replied in a dry, husky voice. "Is one of you my son, Leo?"

"Unfortunately not. But he's in here somewhere. We lost him in the previous labyrinth room."

Orion fell to his knees, putting his hands over his tearful eyes.

137

"Don't be upset, we'll find Leo for you," Marshall consoled.

"These aren't tears of sadness my friends. For eleven years I've been walking these dark caverns hoping for the day when someone would arrive. These are tears of joy. Now tell me, where did you last see my son?"

Sitting down next to Orion, Olly began. "In the previous cave a giant bat picked him up and flew him out of an opening in the cave ceiling. We were helpless and we didn't know what to do."

"Don't worry, my friend."

"Please call me Olly, and this is Marshall."

"Well, Olly and Marshall, I know where they've taken him, those pesky giabats, always on the scavenge for fresh meat. Follow me."

The two boys took Orion's hands and walked through the caves. "What happened to you all those years ago?" Olly asked. "Why couldn't you escape? Who took you down here?"

"Let me tell you what happened," Orion said.

CHAPTER 10

ORION'S STORY

The silence was deafening at the bottom of the ravine. The only sound to break it was the metronomic plummeting drip of water from high above hitting the stone floor.

After knocking himself out from the fall, a seemingly lifeless Orion lay face down on the rock. As water seeped into his mouth he coughed, awakening from his slumber. In an instant he sat upright in a state of complete shock. After checking every limb and part of his body, he was pleasantly surprised to learn he was fine.

His eyes were open, but he couldn't see. He was in pitch darkness as he felt around to find a clue to his location. Shuffling himself across the wet stone floor, he came across something. Moving his hands over the object he soon realised what it was: Victor Golding's body; he hadn't survived the fall.

Orion couldn't believe what was going on. Not long ago, he'd been fishing in his favourite spot, and now his world had turned on its head.

Orion kept feeling around in the darkness, looking for anything that could help, when he struck gold: Victor's rucksack. He reached in and pulled out a torch. Turning it on, it revealed what was left of Victor's body beside him. The fall had disfigured the body beyond recognition and a pool of blood surrounded the head.

Orion took a few deep breaths, trying his best to quell the nauseous feeling in his stomach and clear the black spots that precede a faint. He couldn't believe how Victor looked, while he hardly had a scratch on him. What was going on?

Looking back inside the rucksack he found a knife, compass, some food and drink. Standing up, he shone the torch around hoping to find something else. And there they were: a wooden bow and a quiver full of arrows, which had been freed from Victor's arm during the struggle at the top. Orion slouched back down in a corner of the cave contemplating what to do next. Should he attempt to climb the steep cave wall? Wait for help? Or try to find his own way out through the myriad of tunnels in front of him?

One thing was for sure: he'd never felt so strong and healthy in his life. After a hundred-foot fall, this was an amazing feat.

As Orion was tucking into some food from the rucksack, he heard something not too far away. It sounded like an animal shuffling and scurrying down one of the tunnels. Thinking it was probably a couple of rats wanting a bite of his sandwich, Orion shoved what was left of his snack back into what was now his bag. Standing up, he shone his torch in the direction of the noise.

"Please stop it, it's blinding me," a frail old voice said from inside one of the adjoining tunnels.

Orion moved his torch around, which created a

large shadow of a man. "Who are you?" he demanded, reaching down for the weapons.

"Please turn down the light and I will appear!" the frail voice replied.

Orion pointed the torch down towards the floor, dimming the light in the cave. Slowly the shadow, which had initially appeared large, reduced in size. Out of the far tunnel shuffled a short, hairy man with a branch for a walking stick. His clothes were rags and his grey beard skimmed the ground as he walked. He moved with a limp as one of his legs was made of wood which made a scraping sound on the stone floor. Orion stood there amazed at the vision. "Who are you?" he asked.

The little old man moved closer to him, raised his head and spoke. "My friends call me Stumpy; I live in these caves."

Orion didn't know what was happening and was unsure if he could trust him or not. "What do you want from me?" he said. "Come near me and I'll . . ."

Stumpy interrupted him with a gentle calming voice, "Don't worry, sir, I'm not that kind of person. There is a lot of evil in these caves, but wherever there is evil, there is always some good. No matter how small and frail," he said, gesturing modestly to himself.

Orion sat up. "But what is this place? Where am I? Why me?" he said, agitated.

"Calm down."

"My name's Orion and I don't belong down here, I want my family."

"Well hello, Orion, I'll answer one question at a time," Stumpy said, finding a boulder to sit on. "We are under the town of Brunswick in a labyrinth of caves ruled by creatures of the underworld."

"Oh, well, as long as it's nothing serious," Orion said, shaking his head.

"You were brought here to help steal a large treasure trove which is guarded by a . . ."

"A dragon!" Orion shouted out. "It's a dragon isn't it? I remember my kidnappers mentioning it as I was waking up. I thought they were joking."

Stumpy nodded. "They were correct."

"But what is a dragon slayer?"

"Surely it's self-explanatory."

"I know, a dragon slayer slays dragons. But, what is one?" Orion said.

"You must have been born on the night when a blood moon passed through the constellation of Orion. You must also have drunk the blood of a dragon. That's the reason they kidnapped and dragged you here. They needed you to defeat the dreaded beast."

"Well the constellation of Orion part is right. I remember my mum telling me that was the reason she gave me this name. After that, though, you've lost me. They wanted me to kill a dragon?"

"Look at that," Stumpy said pointing at Orion's neck. "This is your birthmark, correct?"

"Well yes, a bit of an odd-shaped one which got me bullied at school. Why do you ask?"

"Do the three lines remind you of something? A claw mark, perhaps?"

"Er, kind of I suppose," Orion replied.

"Well that's because it is," Stumpy said. "You're reincarnated; the mark is a symbol of how the last dragon slayer died. He was called Tridus and he put up a commendably good fight. The dragon that guards these caves is called Hornbeam. He's been alive for over 5,000 years and many a slayer has succumbed to his power."

"So, what happened to Tridus?" Orion asked.

Laying his hand on Orion's leg, Stumpy continued, "Well the short story is he got sliced from his head and down his neck by Hornbeam's razor-sharp claws. He left an impression on Hornbeam: his name! As they were fighting, Tridus sliced the dragon's horn clean off, leaving a beam of light from his fire, which pierced through the darkness. Since that moment the dragon has been known as Hornbeam."

"How am I meant to defeat Hornbeam, if all before me have failed?"

"Well you can't," Stumpy replied. "I'm sorry, I didn't mean he can't be killed, just that you can't do it on your own."

"What?" Orion blared. "So why did the kidnappers bring me on my own?"

"They didn't know," Stumpy said, with a sigh.

"OK. How do you know?"

Stumpy stood up to answer. "To kill a dragon, you must thrust your sword through its heart. The problem with Hornbeam is that he has two hearts, meaning he's twice as strong and powerful as other dragons. You need two slayers to pierce both hearts at the same time."

Orion slouched forward and put his head in his hands. "Where did you find this out?" he asked.

"Stories are always passed down through the generations of cave trolls, with many dragon slayers trying their best to defeat the mighty beasts. Ethelred, Hector-Wise, Bellafino and Tridus were the slayers I can remember. Hector-Wise was the slayer who found out about its second heart. As he was fighting Hornbeam, he managed to force his sword through the dragon's thick armoured skin. The blade penetrated its heart, but he noticed Hornbeam's chest was still beating from another, much stronger heart. Hornbeam reached out and threw Hector-Wise to the ground, leaving him to die. The slayer's death revitalised the broken beast, healed its heart and gave the dragon another thousand years of life."

"You mentioned Tridus before, the last slayer. Why did he go on his own?" Orion asked.

"He didn't," Stumpy said. "He was with Bellafino. Before Tridus had managed to cut the horn off, Bellafino had succeeded in stabbing Hornbeam through one of his hearts. Unfortunately, Tridus wasn't close enough to do the same to the other heart. Hornbeam swung round, knocking Bellafino against some rocks, causing boulders to crash down on him. That's when, in pure anger, Tridus cut off the dragon's horn. Hornbeam then sliced and killed Tridus, gaining another thousand years of life from the slayer's magical powers."

Orion sat up. "Hang on, what was that about magical powers?" he said.

"You must know," Stumpy replied smiling. "How do you feel?"

"Surprisingly good, seeing that I've just fallen a hundred feet down a ravine. I do feel incredibly strong."

"You will. The closer you get to a dragon the stronger you get. You'll soon start to possess amazing healing powers."

"But I don't want any of this, I want to be at home with my family," Orion said with a tear in his eye. "Is there any way out of here without having to get past Hornbeam?"

"Possibly . . . probably, but that can't happen

now," Stumpy said. "Hornbeam will know you're here; he'll be able to smell your blood. Orion, you have to slay him!"

"What if I don't and just walk away?"

"He'll come after you. Now he knows there's another slayer around, there'll be no stopping him. The dragon needs you, needs the powers you possess . . . you keep him alive! How else do you think he's lived for 5,000 years? Every slayer he eats gives him new life."

"So, I can't walk away, but I can't kill him on my own either?" Orion bemoaned.

"That is true. I'll keep you safe from the dragon for the time being and teach you about the powers you now possess. But until another slayer turns up, we must wait."

"That could be ages!" Orion shouted back.

"It could be decades," Stumpy replied, holding Orion's hand.

"I'm going to die in here then?"

"No," Stumpy replied. "Remember those special powers? They also slow down your ageing process. Believe me, young man. I'll look after you, keep you fed and warm until the time is right. Now let's move on away from here, we don't want to attract attention from anything. We'll go to my cave, there's nothing like bat stew and mushrooms to warm your insides," he said, licking his hairy lips.

Pulling Orion off the boulder, Stumpy walked with the new slayer into the darkness of the caves.

CHAPTER 11

LIKE FATHER, LIKE SON

Orion, Olly and Marshall continued through the maze of caves with the boys enthralled by Orion's story. "Wow, that's amazing," Olly said. "So, where's Stumpy?"

"He'll be in his cave. I'll introduce you all later, but first let's find my son!" Orion replied.

"Yeah, goodness knows what's happened to him," Marshall said.

"Marshall! Don't be disrespectful. I'm sure he's safe, Orion, don't listen to him."

Looking around, Orion laughed, "If he's anything like his father, he'll be just fine."

"You're not worried, then?" Marshall asked.

"Over the past eleven years I've gained some special powers down here. Now, there's a strong chance that Leo will have some of those powers as well, although he may not realise it yet. He'll be OK, trust me."

"Hey, what's that noise?" Olly asked.

"It's the giabats flapping their wings, we're very close," Orion said.

As they looked round a corner, they saw a large cavern filled with hot lava, the rich red and orange hues illuminating the cave. Above they saw hundreds of giabats hanging from the ceiling. "Look!" Olly said. "Over there, it's Leo."

"Oh, my goodness, how did he get up there? He's stuck to the ceiling," Marshall said.

"You two keep a lookout. I'm off to get my son," Orion said.

The two boys stood there, looking over their shoulders like a pair of owls twitching at every slight noise the caves muttered. "You all right, Marshall?" Olly asked. "This is the craziest day ever."

"Yeah, mate I'm fine, a bit strange, but fine. Feels

like days we've been here. What's the time?"

"Getting on for seven o'clock."

"Hopefully our alibis about staying at each other's houses will hold tight."

"We'll be OK. Anyway, my parents will be working," Olly said.

The boys looked up as Orion climbed higher and higher, using every muscle he could muster. "He's like an Olympic athlete," Olly said.

"I know, I wonder if Leo's starting to feel stronger yet?"

"Don't think he feels anything at the moment. He looks like he's stuck to the ceiling with glue or something."

"That'll be guano," Marshall pointed out.

"Guano?" Olly replied. "What's that?"

"Bat poo," Marshall said, laughing. "I've heard tribes use it in the jungles to stick things together, and judging by the size of these giabats they'll produce a lot of it."

"That's disgusting," Olly said, holding his nose. "I do hope Leo's OK though. He doesn't seem to be moving much."

"We'll just have to wait for Orion to bring him down. He's probably just keeping still to pretend he's dead."

"Let's hope so," Olly said. "Hey, did you see that over there?"

Marshall looked round. "Yeah, I see, it's one of those creatures from the maze. They've found us."

"ORION!" both boys bellowed. "Something's coming after us."

"It's a drowner," Orion shouted. "Stay away from it, I'm coming back."

They remained in place until Orion leapt down in front of them. "What do we do?" Olly said, shaking.

Taking an arrow from his quiver, Orion walked up to Marshall. "Hold out your arm," he said.

Marshall straightened his arm and Orion grabbed his sleeve. "Hey what are you doing? You're going to rip it."

"That is exactly what I want to do," Orion said, tearing the sleeve away from Marshall. "Just watch."

Orion wrapped the material around the arrowhead and leaned over, placing it near the lava, causing it to catch fire. The drowner squelched and dripped its way forward, closing in on the boys. "Stay behind me," Orion instructed.

They stood back as Orion took his bow and fired the burning arrow towards the drowner. In a flash the drowner vanished into a cloud of steam.

Marshall walked up to where it once stood, "Take that, Drowner," he said, taking a deep breath to blow it away.

"That was amazing."

"Thanks," Orion replied. "But I must go and rescue my son. Normally if there's one drowner it means the rest aren't far behind, and I haven't got many arrows with me."

Orion sprinted off, but instead of climbing back up the cave walls he jumped on to a giabat as it glided past. Holding its giant wings, he steered it up towards Leo at the roof of the cave.

"Wow, did you just see that, Marshall?" Olly said.

"Yeah, bit of a show off, if you ask me," Marshall replied.

"Ha-ha, are you jealous mate?" Olly joked. "Just accept some people are better at things in life than you."

Looking up, they watched as Orion leapt off the giabat and clung on to a nearby stalactite. He swung like a chimpanzee from one stalactite to the next, eventually making his way to Leo. He prised his unresponsive son away from the guano, placing him over his shoulder.

More giabats appeared with the realisation their dinner was being taken away. That didn't daunt Orion, he simply jumped on them one by one and made his way down them like a giant staircase. He reached the cave floor and strode over to the others. "We need to go quickly," he said.

"Where?" Marshall asked.

"To my friend, Stumpy, he'll be able to help my son."

"Is Leo OK?" Olly asked.

"I think so. I can feel him breathing, but he's unconscious."

With an air of urgency, Orion carried his son through more tunnels and caverns with the two boys following close behind. "Right then, boys," Orion said. "Tell me about yourselves. How come you're here with my son?"

Olly spoke first. "We just wanted to help him. We read about your disappearance all those years ago and realised your son was at our school. It seemed like a good idea at the time!"

Orion nodded. "It was a good idea," he said. "And I thank you again. What about you, Marshall? You look familiar to me."

"I don't see how. I would have been a baby when you vanished. Maybe I've just got one of those familiar faces," Marshall said, with a shrug of his shoulders.

"I suppose you're right, it's so long since I've met other people apart from Stumpy, I'm probably confused."

"Talking of Stumpy, are we near yet?" Olly asked.

"Just round this next bend and we're there."

Rounding the corner, they approached a small opening about three-foot high and lit by something flickering inside. "Stumpy!" Orion said. "Are you in there? Come out, I've got visitors."

A figure appeared in the opening, casting a shadow out towards Orion and the boys. Slowly he hobbled out, his wooden leg scraping along the hard stone floor. "You have waited a long time for this day, Orion," Stumpy said in a soft voice.

"I have," Orion said, laying his son on the floor in front of him. "I need your help more than any other time. It's my son, Leo. These boys came looking for me and the giabats caught him. I rescued him but he's not waking up."

"It's not me that can help young Leo, it's you," Stumpy said. "You've never needed these powers before, but you have them in the palm of your hands.

"What do you mean?" Orion said.

"Place your hands together and concentrate. Channel all your energy into your palms and place them on your son."

Orion put his hands together, shut his eyes and focused. His hands started to glow with a deep orange colour.

"What's going on?" Olly asked.

"No idea, mate, looks like some witchcraft," Marshall replied.

Stumpy turned to the boys. "This is no witchcraft," he said. "A dragon slayer has a power that no witch can replicate . . . the power of life. Orion, place your hands on Leo's head."

Seconds passed with everyone hoping and praying that Leo would recover.

Then a weak voice cried out. "Help!"

"Leo?" Orion shouted. "Leo, can you hear me?"

"Yes, where am I? What's happening? Who are you?" Leo said looking up at a strange man with glowing hands on his head.

"Hi Leo, it's me, your father."

Leo rubbed his eyes and imagined what this man would look like without a full beard and long hair, after all, he'd only seen the picture his mum had shown him. "Dad! It's you."

Leo sat up and grabbed his father, pulling himself in as tight as possible. Everyone else stood motionless for a time as father and son cried with joy at finally being able to look into each other's eyes once again.

"I knew you would find me one day; I've missed you and your mum so much. She is OK, isn't she? The things she must have gone through. And look at you; you're nearly a grown man, with the courage of a lion."

"People kept saying that you'd run away from your

problems, but I knew you'd never leave us on purpose," Leo said, with tears streaming down his face.

"I was kidnapped, my beautiful boy, and soon everybody will know that. First though, I need to tell you all what we must do before we leave."

The boys sat as Orion and Stumpy told them how they had to kill the dragon in order for them to escape, and how Hornbeam would be found guarding the treasure.

"You think I'm a dragon slayer as well?" Leo asked.

Orion glanced down at him, "You're my son, aren't you? My blood is your blood. You might not feel like a slayer yet but wait till you get nearer the dragon."

"Forget about that, I want to see the treasure room," Marshall said.

"Patience, child," Stumpy said. "One will lead to the other, but the important thing is to slay the beast."

"If that's the case, why can't we get to the treasure first?" Marshall said, cheekily.

Orion interrupted. "OK both of you, stop this," he said. "It's getting us nowhere."

"Actually, Dad, I think I'd prefer to find the treasure before confronting the dragon. I'm not exactly prepared to fight yet, am I?" Leo said.

"That's fair enough, we'll go to the treasure cave. But as Stumpy told us, once we're there, Hornbeam won't be far behind."

Stumpy turned around and wandered back towards his cave. "There are a few things in here that might help us," he said. "Leo, can you give me a hand?"

Springing to his feet, Leo enthused, "Yeah sure, I'm coming."

Crouching down, Leo entered Stumpy's cave. Inside, it appeared to be like a normal home but a lot smaller. In the corner was a wood burner supplying the heat and cooking a large stew, which was bubbling away on top. Against the other wall was a small but cosy-looking bed covered in a large fur blanket.

"Leo!" Stumpy called. "Come through here."

Leo made his way towards Stumpy, being careful not to bang his head on the low ceiling. He couldn't believe his eyes. "Where did you get those from?" he asked.

Stumpy was holding two large swords, shining and glistening as if they'd just been forged. "These are the weapons of a dragon slayer," Stumpy replied. "You and your father will need these to defeat Hornbeam."

"But where did you get them?" Leo asked again.

"My forefathers. Over many thousands of years, slayers have tried and failed to kill this mighty beast. The swords are the only remains of those great warriors," Stumpy said, raising one of the weapons. "This one was from the mighty Tridus. He was the one who severed the horn."

"Let me try with that one please."

Stumpy hobbled over to Leo and passed him the sword.

"It's not as heavy as it looks," Leo said, surprised.

He received a smile in return. "Oh, but it is, young man, it's the dragon slayer powers. You're getting stronger without realising it. Your father was right, you are a slayer."

Leo lifted the sword above his head. "I can feel it now. I feel the power!"

Stumpy passed Leo the other sword. "Your father

will need this one, it was Bellafino's sword. He was another great slayer."

"Thanks, but I've just realised something. If I'm getting stronger doesn't that mean . . ."

"Yes!" Stumpy said. "Hornbeam's getting closer and must be aware we're here."

Stumpy led Leo out of the cave to re-join the others. "Dad! Look, I'm getting stronger; I can lift this sword."

"I told you, we'll make a slayer out of you yet," Orion said, taking the other sword.

"Come on, everyone," Stumpy said. "I don't want Hornbeam knowing where I live. The sooner we get to the treasure room the better."

As they walked through the caves, Orion and Leo practised with their swords, majestically swinging them through the air, causing shimmers of light to appear in the torchlight reflections. With every thrust and block of the weapons, the slayers grew in confidence. They both began to move like champion swordsmen, each impressive strike retaliated with a greater block.

"You two are getting good at this," Olly said.

"Hope you can sort Hornbeam out, otherwise we've all had it."

"They'll be fine," Stumpy said, nodding his hairy head. "Slayers are always in this position. You can't practise against a dragon, can you? When the time comes, they'll know what to do."

"Well, I'll believe it when I see it," Marshall said. "If you ask me, we're better off grabbing some treasure and escaping as fast as we can."

"Now Hornbeam can sense we're all here, he'll track down the slayers wherever they go," Stumpy replied. "There's no other option but to defeat him. Right here, right now."

"Hey look!" Olly said, pointing his torch in front of him. "We've found it."

CHAPTER 12

THE TREASURE CAVE

The treasure cave shone like a distant fairground in the night. Even from afar they could see the gold, green and red hues of all the precious stones' shimmering reflections. Everybody's footsteps speeded up; they couldn't wait to get inside.

"Wow, this is amazing. So many colours," Olly said, entering the cave.

"We're rich!" Marshall shouted, prising some of the jewels away from the wall.

Orion followed behind the boys, running with Stumpy and Leo under his arms. "Turn that torch off, now," Orion ordered.

"Why? What's wrong?" Olly asked.

"Drowners, loads of them!" Leo said.

"Hopefully they won't know we've come in here. Everyone stay still," Orion said.

The cave fell silent. The only noise was the drowners, squelching and dripping as they drew closer. Marshall nudged Orion. "Can't you use your bow and arrow again?" he whispered.

"There are too many of them. Anyway, there's no lava nearby to light the arrows."

Leo began clenching his fists and bending his elbows. "What are you doing?" Olly asked.

"I'm getting stronger by the minute, mate. My muscles are huge. Shall we try and get them, Dad?"

Orion looked over, "No chance; strength holds no power against those drowners. Once you touch them, their bodies suck you in and that's it. They drown you in their own liquid."

"Listen," Stumpy said, tapping his stick for attention. "Can you hear it?"

"I can hear what sounds like a waterfall coming towards us," Marshall joked.

"No, not the drowners. The footsteps."

Everyone listened. Stumpy was correct. There was a distant thud getting louder and louder. Suddenly across the opening of the treasure cave, a giant wall of fire blazed by.

Hornbeam was here.

The fire engulfed the drowners, instantaneously turning them into steam. The boys didn't know whether to be happy or sad: they were rid of the drowners, but would Hornbeam find them?

Silence resumed as everyone stood still, watching a giant creature stride across the cave entrance. They couldn't even see the top of its immense size. One giant foot after another went past, eventually followed by a thick, long tail covered in green scales. It swished from side to side.

"He's massive," Leo said, shaking.

"Quiet!" Stumpy said as he listened to Hornbeam's retreating footsteps. "I think we're safe now. The drowners must have distracted him from sensing us. Hopefully he's gone back to his nest."

"His nest?" Marshall said. "He's not a bird."

"He *is* a bird!" Stumpy snapped back. "A giant bird which weighs more than a truck, has ten-inch claws like a Tyrannosaurus Rex, is covered in armour, and breathes fire. Believe me, I know everything there is to know about this monster, so respect him and respect me. Do I make myself clear?"

"Yeah, suppose so," Marshall muttered back.

Olly explored the cave by torchlight.

"Look over there," Leo said, grabbing his dad by the arm. "It's a skeleton."

"I don't know who that could be," Orion replied.

"I know!" Olly said. "It's George Bumble, the ghost we talked to earlier. He said he was murdered here by that Golding fellow. This is where it all began, the arguments over the money and the treasure, the reason why the creatures from the underworld took over these caves. It all happened here."

"It sure did!" Marshall said. "And it's not the only thing that's going to happen here."

"What are you going on about now?" Olly joked.

Bending down to unzip his rucksack, Marshall reached inside and pulled out a gun.

"What the heck are you doing, mate? Put it down! Where did you get that?" Olly shouted.

Marshall lifted the gun, pointing it towards the group, "Right, all of you stand against that back wall where I can see you."

Orion raised his arms. "OK, we'll do what you say, just don't pull that trigger. You don't want to hurt anyone."

"Why not?" Marshall snapped back. "Why don't I want to hurt the person who killed my father? This is my Uncle Lance's gun. He gave it to me to get back what's ours!"

"What?" Olly said, in disbelief. "Orion's not a murderer. We've come here to find him . . ."

"You wanted to get revenge; this is all your own doing, isn't it?" said Leo.

"Correct, smart boy," Marshall said. "Orion threw my father, Victor Golding, off the rope bridge and left him to die, leaving my mum and Uncle Lance to bring me up."

Orion stood forward. "Your father kidnapped me along with your Uncle Lance!" he shouted. "I had no choice but to kill him."

"So, let's get this straight," Olly said, with his legs shaking. "You're related to the people who kidnapped

Orion . . . you're Drake Golding's great-grandson?"

"Well you did wonder what the letter G stood for in my middle name. It's Golding. I'm James Golding Marshall and I'm going to have what my family's been due for decades. My Uncle Lance, who escaped the clutches of Orion, told me everything I needed to know. I just needed to hatch a plan to get down here, find Orion and take the treasure."

Olly couldn't believe what he was hearing. "The newspaper clipping you found, did you really just find it?"

"Course not!" Marshall said. "My mum kept everything about Orion's disappearance when it happened. She knew he'd killed her husband. It was only a matter of time before I could use it to help her and my family seek revenge."

"And the locket? The fishing reel?" Leo asked.

"Ha-ha!" Marshall laughed. "Well, I had to lead you down the right path, or was that the right tunnel?"

"No wonder you pretended not to see the cube in the water tank. You were scared George Bumble's ghost might have seen who you are," Leo said.

"I should have realised too," said Orion. "I thought I recognised you. It was the eyes; you've the same as your dad's. It was that stare he gave me just before I pushed him off that bridge."

"Yes, and if you keep on talking like that it'll be my eyes that'll be the last thing you see before you die. Do you understand?" Marshall said, his finger twitching on the trigger.

"How come you didn't bring your Uncle Lance with you on this revenge mission of yours?" Orion asked.

"He couldn't face coming back here after what you did to his brother. He's been scared of the dark, and claustrophobic ever since. Luckily I'm here to avenge all that."

"So, young boy," Stumpy said calmly, shuffling closer to Marshall. "What are you going to do now? Shoot us all? Get past Hornbeam on your own and then try and find your way back out of these caves alive?"

Marshall looked at Stumpy. "Course not. Clearly you think I haven't thought this through. I admit I wasn't expecting you to join the party. Anyway, I

170

think that has worked out in my favour."

Marshall pointed the gun towards Stumpy and with a quick pull of the trigger, fired a shot at him.

"No!" Orion shouted.

"Stay back all of you," Marshall warned. "Anyone helps and they'll be joining him."

Stumpy lay on the floor with blood seeping through his tattered clothes. The bullet had gone into his chest, but he was still breathing. "Now, Orion and Leo," Marshall said, directing his gun towards them. "You are going to kill this dragon for me. If not, Leo, your mum will die."

"What?" Leo screamed. "Not my mum, leave her out of this."

"I will. If you and your dad do what I say."

"There is a slight problem with your plan," Orion interjected.

"What?"

"Hornbeam, we don't know where he is. The only one who knows is lying on the ground, fighting for his life."

Marshall walked along and addressed Stumpy, simultaneously tapping his wooden leg, "Now then, old man. We're going to do a deal, all right? You're going to tell us where we can find Hornbeam's lair, and in return Orion will use his healing powers on you when we get back."

Stumpy slowly opened his eyes. "Out of this cave . . . follow the lava flow back to the centre of the volcano," he said in a resigned voice.

"A volcano?"

"Yes, we are in a living, breathing volcano. It was once dormant, but the underworld has reignited its flames."

"And we'll find Hornbeam there?"

"Yes," Stumpy said, closing his eyes.

"Don't worry, Stumpy!" Orion said. "We'll be back as quick as we can. Hold on."

"Olly!" Marshall said. "You stay here with Stumpy. Orion and Leo, you're coming with me. You've got a dragon to kill!"

Bending down, Olly reached into his rucksack for the first aid kit. He put some cotton wool on Stumpy's wound and wrapped a bandage around his small frame. Draping his jacket over him to keep warm, he said. "Keep strong, little man. We need you."

CHAPTER 13

THE HUNT FOR HORNBEAM

"Stumpy will be OK, won't he?" Leo asked, following his dad and Marshall out of the treasure cave.

"As long as you're quick killing Hornbeam, he'll be fine," Marshall said.

"Still can't believe you lied about everything to get us down here."

"Well believe it, because it's happening. I want back what belongs to my family. If I have to lie to get it, well that's tough."

Orion turned around. "You two kids arguing will

not help the situation," he said. "Leo, just do what he says, and Marshall, you expect us to kill a dragon for you, a dragon that has been around and killed many a slayer before we turned up, so let us concentrate on our mission. If we don't succeed, Hornbeam will be having you next. Do you understand?"

"Well, you have a point, but just remember I'm in charge," Marshall said. "Now let's find this lava flow Stumpy told us about."

Orion held Leo's hand while Marshall, still aiming his gun, followed them as they walked down the damp, dark tunnel which Hornbeam had passed through.

"Hey, Dad! I think I can see it getting lighter down there. It's getting hotter too."

"You're right, we must be getting close to the lava. Stay close to me, there's more than just a dragon down here."

As the three of them progressed, the tunnel lightened until they saw what they were looking for. "It's the lava!" Marshall said. "So which way are we meant to go?"

"Well if Hornbeam's at the source of the volcano

and lava runs away from it, then we follow where it's come from," Orion said.

"You don't have to sound so patronising," Marshall replied.

"Hey, did either of you see that?" Leo said.

"Don't try to distract me with your little games," Marshall said. "It was probably a shadow."

"You're right, Marshall, it was a shadow. Unfortunately, it's not one of ours!"

"What do you mean?"

"They're called shadow stalkers. They scurry around in the dim light of the caves mimicking people's shadows so they can get close to them."

"What happens when they get close?" Leo asked, gripping his father's arm.

"They move up your body to your face and suffocate you."

"Blimey!" Marshall gulped. "How do we stop them? Turn off all the lights?"

"Not a bad idea, but with this lava running through here it's impossible to be in complete darkness. Hang on a minute, I remember Stumpy telling me that giabats feed on them by sucking them up off the ground."

"Well that doesn't help us at the moment, does it?" Marshall moaned as he looked up to check whether any giabats were gliding about.

"I know!" Leo shouted. "If we smell like giabats, those shadow stalkers will leave us alone."

Marshall looked perplexed, "And how are we meant to smell like them?"

Leo bent down and scooped up some giabat guano. "With this!" he said, rubbing and smearing it over his clothes.

"Great idea." Orion beamed.

"You have got to be kidding me," Marshall said.

"No, we're not," Orion said. "And you'd better get some on you because I can see a shadow stalker heading your way. And I don't want them anywhere near Leo or me."

Marshall spun around to see a shadow moving over the rocks towards him. He picked up some guano and smeared it over his clothes. "This is disgusting," he said.

"But it's working. Look!" Leo shouted in glee.

As if by magic, the shadow stalker slowed, scenting a nearby giabat. Then it turned away and scurried back towards the rocks. "Thank goodness for that!" Marshall sighed. "Now let's get on with the job in hand."

The three of them walked adjacent to the lava river, hoping to come across its source and find the dragon's nest. The lava gave off an excruciating heat, bubbles exploding only feet away from them, but they knew it was the only way.

"I know I should feel tired and hot, but I feel amazing at the moment," Leo said. "Watch this, Dad."

Running over to the cave wall, Leo jumped and somersaulted over it, landing safely back to the ground. "Very good, Leo, your slayer powers are improving. Stumpy told me once, slayers can each possess different powers."

"Like what, Dad?"

"Well, anything from fighting skills and athleticism to mind control and healing powers."

"Wow! So, what can you do?"

"Well, since I've been down here, I've become a lot stronger and can climb walls with ease. I'm also good with a sword and of course I'm an excellent archer."

"I hope I can do all those things," Leo said.

"I'm sure you can, Son. You'll have individual powers as well, but you won't realise what they are until you have to use them."

"Yeah, yeah, come on you two, stop yapping," Marshall said striding ahead. "You can get to know each other later. Now, let's find this dragon."

Back in the treasure cave, Olly was still looking after Stumpy.

"I didn't trust him the moment I saw him," Stumpy said.

"Sshhh!" Olly said. "You're meant to be resting. Is there anything I can get you?"

Stumpy held Olly's hand, "I'm fine, just keep me warm and watered. They haven't got far to go to Hornbeam. Let's just hope the two slayers defeat the mighty dragon."

"They will, won't they?"

"With all the powers they hold, Hornbeam should be gone forever."

"What if . . ."

"What if Hornbeam wins? His strength will be revitalised, to rule the underworld for many more millennia."

Putting his head in his hands, Olly wailed, "I want to go home, Stumpy. I miss my family and my dog, and I wish I'd never agreed to find Leo's dad."

"But you did," Stumpy said reaching up to touch Olly. "You're a good person; a kind and loving young man who'll do anything for a friend in need. What has happened, you couldn't possibly have foreseen. One thing's for sure, I'll do everything in my power to help you."

"Thanks, Stumpy, but you're not much use to anyone in your predicament."

Looking up, Stumpy noticed something reflecting in the firelight. "Don't worry, I may be wounded, but I might still be able to help. See that orange stone high up on the wall, just above that ledge?" he said, pointing his stick. "Could you get it for me, please?"

Walking over, Olly began the climb. He clambered up towards the stone and sat perilously on the ledge, trying to grab it. "It's stuck solid. It won't move."

"It's been there for thousands of years, young

man, of course it's going to be hard to get out," Stumpy said, trying not to laugh through the pain.

Reaching into his pocket, Olly pulled out his penknife, releasing the biggest blade on it. He scraped away at the rock, revealing more of the mysterious orange stone. He managed to wrap his hand around it and tugged with all his might, pulling the gem away from the wall. "Got it, Stumpy!" he said.

"Good boy, now bring it to me."

Rushing back over, Olly passed the stone to the frail old man. "What is it? What does it do?" he asked.

"This is called magnazite, a stone forged over a thousand years from volcanoes. Its other name is Dragon's Curse."

Olly looked puzzled. "How will this help?"

"Watch this."

Stumpy dropped the magnazite into the fire and within a split second the fire extinguished.

"Wow!" Olly said, relighting the fire. "That's amazing. Sorry for being a bit slow here, but how is that going to help the situation?"

Stumpy gave a grin. "Hornbeam's main weapon is fire. If it consumes any of these gemstones, we'll have a dragon without a fire in its belly."

"I get it, although Orion and Leo will be too far away now. What should we do?"

"Slayers have many strengths and powers. Orion is strong, agile and a great archer, but I don't know about Leo yet. I can see he's strong. I'm hoping he possesses something the slayer Bellafino had."

"And what was that?"

"Telepathy," Stumpy replied.

"Tele what?"

"Telepathy; a way of using your mind to communicate."

"That sounds awesome. But hang on, even if he does have this telepathy thing, how do we get in touch with him?"

Stumpy gave a few coughs. Wincing with pain, he slowly sat up, "I'm going to tell you something now, something which I haven't told anyone for years, including Orion."

"Go on," Olly said, intrigued.

"When I first met Orion, after he'd fallen down

181

into the caves, I told him a few stories about previous slayers who had tried to defeat Hornbeam. One of those tales was about Bellafino, who was crushed under rocks and boulders the dragon had thrown at him."

"What an awful way to die!" Olly said.

"Well that's it, he didn't die. Well, not entirely."

"Where is he?"

"Young Olly . . . you're speaking to him!"

"What! You're Bellafino?"

"I am. Well, at least what's left of him."

Olly was confused. "So how come you're still alive? I know you survived the crush but surely you're hundreds of years old."

"I am indeed. I sold my soul to the God of the Underworld. He came to me whilst taking my last breath, offering to let me live in peace as a guardian of the underworld if I left the mighty Hornbeam alone. I wasn't in any state to argue so I agreed. I couldn't tell Orion as he would have wanted me to fight Hornbeam with him. But the God of the Underworld stripped away my fighting abilities and replaced them with longevity of life; I still get old, but at a much slower rate."

Olly looked astounded. "So, are you dead or alive then?"

"I feel alive, I can still breathe, but my soul has gone. If they manage to defeat Hornbeam I will be no more in this land. Until the underworld is summoned once again."

"You can't leave us all down here, we need you."

"I'll give Orion and Leo this one last piece of knowledge, that's all the help you will need."

"But what if we ever need to find you again?" Olly said through his tears.

"There is one way to get to the underworld; through a pyramid portal."

Suddenly a gigantic roar bellowed through the network of caves, vibrating the walls.

"Enough of this talk, we're running out of time," Stumpy said.

"You mentioned you lost some of your powers. Do you still have some?"

"Yes, I too possess the power of telepathy."

"Well, what are we waiting for?"

Stumpy shut his eyes, entering a state of deep thought and blocking the pain from the bullet wound. *Leo? Leo, can you hear me?* he called with his mind.

"Aaarrgghh!" Leo shouted.

"What's wrong?" Orion asked.

"I just heard someone in my head."

Don't worry, it's me Stumpy. I'm talking to you through our minds. Don't speak, just say things to me in your head. I will hear them.

Hi, it's Leo, he thought with trepidation.

Hello, you've just discovered another slayer power, telepathy. It is one that only a few slayers possess.

This is so strange.

Are you at Hornbeam's lair yet? Stumpy asked, concentrating hard.

No, but we must be getting close as I'm feeling stronger and getting new powers.

I've got to tell you something. If you see any orange gemstones in the rocks, use them to help defeat it; they will extinguish the dragon's fire.

Er, OK. We'll keep a look out. Thank you, Stumpy.

No, thank you, young Leo. Good luck to you and your father.

"You all right, Leo?" Marshall said, thumping his arm.

"Yes, I've just been in touch with Stumpy through telepathy; it's a special power I've got."

"I knew you'd have other powers," Orion said. "What did Stumpy want?"

"He wanted us to look out for orange gemstones. He said they'd help put the dragon's fire out."

Putting his arm around Leo, Orion said proudly, "Well done Son, that will help us so much. Hornbeam's fire could kill us all in one breath."

Marshall, Orion and Leo continued their search for the gigantic dragon as they followed the lava river to its source, which at times was becoming treacherous even for the athletic slayers. Large boulders blocked the easy routes, forcing them on to their bellies to either climb over or crawl through the smallest gaps.

"This is crazy," Marshall moaned. "It's all right for you two, but I haven't got any powers to help me."

"Go back if you can't handle it," Orion said.

"Hey, can you hear that?" Leo said. "It sounds like a waterfall."

Marshall walked ahead, with his gun still pointing at the slayers, he glanced around the corner and replied, "Wow! It is. Well kind of, anyway."

"What do you mean, kind of?" Leo said.

"Well, it's a waterfall without water!"

Catching up with Marshall, they both had a look for themselves. Before them, gushing down the rocks, was a hundred-foot cascade of molten lava.

"This is unbelievable," Orion said. "It's the source of the lava river; it's a lavafall!"

"You mean we're here?" Marshall asked.

"Think so, this is what Stumpy told us anyway."

"The centre of the volcano," Leo said with a gulp.

"Yes, this is where Hornbeam's lair will be. Be on your guard both of you and stay close to each other."

"I'll make the decisions, Orion," Marshall said, with a shake in his voice. "You two lead the way."

The three of them wandered around the lavafall, looking for clues as to where Hornbeam might be. Skeletons of creatures which had come to a very hot and sudden end were visible on the ground. Huge giabats flew high in the cave, gliding on the warm thermals produced by the lava below.

"Look up there!" Leo shouted through the noise of the lavafall.

"Yeah, we can see the giabats," Marshall said.

"No, look at the ceiling of the cave. There's something flickering orange."

"Yes, Leo," Orion said. "They might be the gemstones Stumpy told you to collect."

Looking up, a beam of light gradually moved across the cave. Orion put his arms across both boys.

"Don't make a sound," Orion whispered. "I think it's Hornbeam. He's here somewhere!"

The beam of light was coming from behind the lavafall, sporadically cutting through the falling molten lava. An almighty roar shook the caves, proving without doubt, the presence of the almighty dragon.

"Do you think he knows we're here, Dad?"

"I think so. He'll be able to smell a slayer from there."

"So, what's the plan?" Marshall asked Orion.

"I'm not sure yet, I've not really done anything like

this before. Haven't you got any ideas, Marshall? After all you're the reason we're here, aren't you?"

"My plan is for you to sort out the dragon or else you and your family will get killed. Is that a clear enough plan for you?"

Orion looked at Leo and smiled. "Nothing is going to harm my family; I've waited too long to see them all again. Are you ready for this, Leo?"

"Ready as I'll ever be, Dad."

"Right then. Marshall, first you will have to get out of the way."

"Thought I had to stay close to you guys?"

"Please do what I say," Orion said. "As much as I hate you, I know we have to keep you alive down here. See that alcove over there? Go and hide in it until we're finished."

Marshall ran over to the small cave while Orion and Leo composed themselves for the forthcoming battle. Both slayers had the swords Stumpy had given them slotted down their belts, while Orion, with his quiver full of arrows, clutched his bow.

They walked out into full view of the lavafall, waiting for Hornbeam to see them. The beam of light appeared again, pulsing through the lava and circulating around the vast cave. The light travelled frantically, searching for the slayers. Orion and Leo stood there like beacons, glowing brightly in the darkness of the cave as Hornbeam's light came to an abrupt halt. The dragon had found the slayers it needed to sustain its life for another 2,000 years.

"Let's keep moving," Orion said. "It's our only way to avoid it."

"OK . . . I love you, by the way."

"And I love you. I knew we'd find each other again, just not in these circumstances."

"Look! Look at the lavafall!" Leo shouted.

Looking towards where he was pointing, Orion saw it bulging forwards; forming into the shape of a dragon. Increasing in size, the bulge showed glimpses of dark-green scales as the molten lava dripped off the monster.

Hornbeam gave out an almighty roar. It echoed through the cave system, setting off mini-landslides and dislodging boulders which had stood there for thousands of years. With a few flaps of his giant wings, he cleared the lavafall with the remaining molten lava falling like water off a duck's back.

With the two slayers looking on, Hornbeam breathed out a giant ball of fire which raced towards them. Jumping in opposite directions, they tried to confuse the mighty beast.

Orion fired a few arrows. But they just bounced off Hornbeam's thick, armoured skin.

The heat was intense with steam shooting up from wells deep below the ground. Hornbeam became distracted and partially blinded by the mist, so Leo climbed up one of the cave walls.

"Be careful!" Orion shouted.

"Don't worry, Dad. I've got a plan."

Leo climbed as high as he could, every muscle in his body bulging as he gripped the wet stone. Looking around, he fervently hoped to get close to what would help him. There it was, a giabat, gracefully gliding on the warm air thermals. Its wingspan was at least four metres with a body the size of a small child.

Leo saw his opportunity and took it.

The creature released a piercing shriek at unexpected shock of Leo landing on its back.

Leo grabbed its long pointy ears to steady himself, stroked its body and thought hard, trying to use his newfound slayer power on the giabat in an attempt to calm it down and gain control. *I'm your friend, I won't hurt you.* The giabat gracefully nodded its head and let Leo take command.

Gliding in circles above Hornbeam's lair, Leo shouted, "Hey Dad! Look at me!"

"I see you, but watch out. I think something else has spotted you."

Through the mist, a beam of light pointed vertically up towards the giabat, followed by a fireball.

Leo pulled one of the giabat's ears, causing it to tilt to one side, narrowly missing the flames. Leo knew he couldn't hang around in his present position for too much longer, so he steered the giabat into the warm air from the remnants of the fire, making it rise to the top of the cave.

He saw what he had been searching for – an orange gemstone moulded into the rock.

He pulled out his sword, jabbing at the stone. Pieces of rock fell away, leaving enough room to get a grip on the orange gem. With huge effort to avoid losing his balance, Leo yanked the gemstone free and shouted, "I've got it!"

"You've got what?"

"One of those orange gems Stumpy told me about. Once I throw it down to you, tie it to one of your arrows and shoot it into Hornbeam's mouth."

"I'll try my best. Well done."

Leo dropped the gem through the foggy air into Orion's hand. Fastening it to one of his arrows, he waited for the dragon to appear through the mist. As the haze lifted, Orion saw something coming towards him. He crouched down, slowly pulling back the arrow.

"No Dad, don't fire! It's me."

"Leo!"

"Hey, thought you might need some help down here."

"Very funny! You know you almost had an arrow flying towards you."

Jumping off the giabat, Leo stood beside his father. They both peered through the mist, focusing on the silhouette of the dragon's outstretched wings.

Hornbeam was ready, but so were the slayers.

"This is going to be tricky. I only have one shot at this."

"You can do it. Just wait until he's about to breathe fire, then shoot."

Hornbeam started a slow flap of its giant wings, causing the mist to create mini-tornadoes on either side of it. As the wings beat faster, the wind collected debris and small boulders, then launched them all over the cave, narrowly avoiding hitting the slayers.

Suddenly Hornbeam took off, heading towards them. The dragon drew nearer with every flap, as Orion pulled back his arrow ready for the opportune moment.

"Now!" Leo shouted.

Letting go, Orion watched the arrow soar through the cave. Hornbeam, in full flight, opened his ferocious jaws and released another cascade of fire.

The arrow zoomed nearer, but to Orion's disbelief, it skimmed over the top of the beast and implanted in the cave wall.

"Nooo!" Orion screamed.

"Dad, move!" Leo cried out, watching the fire heading straight towards them.

Orion somersaulted over the fire and landed on a ledge. "You OK? I'm sorry I missed. It must have been the extra weight of the gem . . . Leo? Are you there?"

Everything was silent for a few seconds as Orion searched. Looking up, an object whizzed past Orion's head.

"I'm fine!" Leo shouted, hanging on to another giabat. "Just distract Hornbeam. I'll be back soon."

Orion jumped around the cave firing arrows and, when he was close enough, stabbing the dragon with his sword. It was evident that Hornbeam was tiring. Every flight and movement he made was taking its toll on his 5,000-year-old body.

Leo noticed this as he looked down on the beast and knew he had to act quickly. Guiding the giabat towards the wall where the arrow attached to the gem was lodged, he reached forward and pulled it out. As Leo turned around, Hornbeam lowered his wings and stopped fighting – probably to recover some strength. This was the perfect opportunity.

Leo leaned forward on the giabat, urging it go faster, and aimed for Hornbeam. As he approached, he swung to the side, one arm dangling down and holding the arrow.

Hornbeam sensed something was coming towards him. Just as the giant turned its head round, Leo was there and he forced the arrow, attached to the orange gem, into the hole where Hornbeam's horn had once been.

The dragon released an incredible roar, causing rocks and boulders to dislodge throughout the caves. Hornbeam flew away from the slayers.

Jumping off the giabat to join his dad, Leo asked, "Do you think it's worked? He seems to be in a lot of pain."

Orion hugged his son. "Hopefully, my little man, we'll soon see."

In the distance they watched the beast rear up on his back legs in preparation for breathing more fire. Taking a deep breath, he opened his giant jaws and . . . nothing! Not even a spark or a flicker of fire came out. Even more noticeable was that his beam had fizzled out like an extinguished candle.

"We've done it, Dad," Leo said, smiling like a Cheshire cat.

"Not quite. He could easily strike us down with those giant claws."

"Well, it looks like we might be getting some help!"

Over in the distance, creatures of the underworld crept out of every nook and cranny. Drowners and shadow stalkers approached the dragon, safe in the knowledge the fire couldn't kill them.

Orion and Leo stood their ground, watching in amazement as the shadow stalkers glided up the scaly, hard skin of the dragon's tail and on to its back. Drowners squelched up to its legs, only to be kicked away with its last remaining ounce of energy.

Hornbeam stretched out his wings with another roar, but this time it was one of pain.

The shadow stalkers had reached his head and were starting to suffocate him.

Orion saw his chance. Reaching for his arrows, he fired and managed to pin Hornbeam's wings like a butterfly to the cave wall, "This is it . . . are you ready?"

"I'm a slayer, aren't I? Of course I'm ready."

Striding towards the helpless animal, the slayers

jumped on to its knees. In unison, they leapt up towards its immense chest, pulling swords out of their belts. Together, they thrust them deep into both of Hornbeam's hearts.

A harrowing noise erupted from the giant beast, making the whole cave system shake and crumble. "Quick, Leo, jump down and follow me!" Orion said, running towards a small alcove.

"Is that it? Have we done it?" Leo said, panting.

"Looks like it. Hornbeam appears to be changing."

Looking on, they could both see the dragon growing brighter and brighter, until what seemed to be a million golden dragonflies burst from its body. They floated into the atmosphere before dispersing into smoke.

Hornbeam was no more. The guardian of the treasure cave, put there by George Bumble to keep out Drake and his family, was gone forever. Once Hornbeam was dead, the rest of the creatures returned to the underworld. The giabats vanished, the shadow stalkers and drowners disappeared, never to haunt those tunnels and caves again. Even the lavafall turned into rock as it ceased its endless flow.

"We're free, Dad! Nothing can stop us getting out of here now," Leo said, jubilantly.

A loud clapping noise came out from one of the small caves. "Well, well," Marshall said. "First, I must congratulate you both. I didn't think you had it in you to kill something like that."

"We didn't have a choice, Marshall. It was either us and our friends, or the dragon," Orion replied. "Anyway, we've done what you wanted us to do. We've killed Hornbeam. Now you can escape with your precious treasure."

"So you did," Marshall nodded. "But let's all get back to the treasure cave, I've got something to share with you all."

Orion pointed at Marshall. "We'll go back to the treasure room as our friend is there and we have to save Stumpy, not because you want us to. OK, Marshall?"

"You'll both do what I say!" Marshall said, pointing the gun at Leo.

"Just go along with him, Dad. It's not worth the risk of getting hurt," Leo said.

Orion took his young son's hand and they walked

away from where the lava had once flowed. Marshall followed close behind them; an annoying grin spread across his face. He knew that his plan was coming together.

CHAPTER 14

THE SLAYER'S RETURN

They walked through the maze of tunnels in near darkness. No light emanated from the lava flow and the glowing creatures were nowhere to be seen. All they had was Leo's torch which was now running low on batteries, and of course Orion's knowledge of the tunnels.

Eventually, Marshall, Orion and Leo made it back to the treasure room. Leo was the first one to enter as he couldn't wait to tell Stumpy what had happened. "Stumpy! Stumpy!" he shouted.

"He's gone," Olly said, sitting alone in the corner.

"I was talking with him . . . then he just faded away."

"Of course," Orion said. "He was part of it all; when the afterlife left then so did he. I wish I'd had a chance to thank him for looking after me all those years."

"He did say thank you and that he hopes to see us all again someday."

"I hope we do. He had some great stories to tell," Orion said.

"He sure did," Olly replied. "He had just finished telling me about his greatest story when he disappeared."

"What was it?" Leo asked.

"Enough of this," Marshall interrupted. "What do you think this is, story time or something? If you want to hear Stumpy's tales so much you can all join him."

Marshall lifted his gun and aimed it at Leo.

Grabbing the bow and an arrow, Orion fired, but it veered off hopelessly wide of Marshall. Even Leo went to pick up a large boulder to throw at him but struggled to move it.

"You fools," Marshall laughed. "Don't you see?

You've killed Hornbeam; the one and only thing that gave you all those powers. You're the same as everybody else now . . . normal!"

Olly and Leo looked scared as Marshall waved his gun at them all.

"You're not a murderer, Marshall," Orion reasoned. "Just take what you want and get on your way."

"As if you're going to let me get away with all this. Now turn around all of you and face the wall. I'd prefer to shoot you when you're not staring at me."

Orion, Leo and Olly shuffled their feet around until they faced the cave wall. With tears in his eyes, Olly once more begged Marshall to stop, "Please don't do this, you won't be in trouble. I thought we were friends? I don't even know why you got me involved in all this."

"Ha, well that was more luck than judgement to be honest. I knew I had to get Leo down here, but also knew he wouldn't go with just me. Luckily my mum saw my school year photo and recognised the name Olly Webber. The son of the student nurse who, all those years ago, got my great-grandfather Drake

Golding into trouble for stealing from the hospital. It caused him no end of problems and was to blame for his deterioration of health . . . costing him his life. After I found out that information all I had to do was to get friendly with you and convince you to help Leo. It's funny how things always work out, isn't it?"

"Wow, you really are the lowest of the low, Marshall. You got me involved because of something my parents did before I was even born. You're pathetic. I really hope you don't get away with this," Olly said, with anger pouring out of him.

"Too late," Marshall said as he cocked his gun.

Waiting for the inevitable, Orion clutched his son's hand when there was an enormous thud.

"What was that?" Leo said, shaking.

Orion turned around to see Marshall face down in a cloud of dust, "Guys, we're saved. Someone's knocked Marshall out."

They spun round and saw two vague shadows through the cloud of dust. Slowly it dispersed, leaving a familiar sight.

"Jessica? Is that really you?" Olly shouted with glee.

"It sure is, Olly, thought you might need some help!"

In front of them stood Olly's sister, her boyfriend Sam, and best of all, Madison, who pounded over to Olly, jumping up to lick him all over. "Oh Maddy! I've missed you so much," Olly said, crying. "But Jess, how did you find us down here?"

"Well, you promised to ring me later on in the day, but you didn't."

"I'm sorry, but as you can see there isn't much need for a phone box down here."

"No, but there is one at the edge of the woods! Anyway, don't worry, we're here now. It was getting late and I remembered you saying that you were meeting up with Marshall at his house. Sam and I went up to the house to find out if his mum knew where you all were. We knocked and rang the bell but to no avail, so we thought we'd have a peek through some of the windows, you know, just in case. You'll never guess what we saw?"

"Believe me, Jess, after what's happened to us, nothing could surprise me."

"Well, we looked through Marshall's bedroom

window around the back of the house. On the walls were scraps of newspaper with headlines about Orion going missing and a noticeboard displayed what appeared to be a plan about a tunnel. It had Leo's name on it, and yours too."

Olly nodded his head. "Yeah, unfortunately we found that out on the way. It was all a plan. Marshall and his family knew what they were going to do even before I knew him. But how did you find the tunnel in all of the forest?"

"There was only one thing that could help us find you and the tunnel, so we rushed back home and got Madison. She could sniff your scent from a mile away and is used to running through the forest; it was a no brainer."

"Amazing!" Olly said proudly, giving his loyal friend another cuddle. "Hang on, though, how did you get over the ravine? The bridge had collapsed when we tried."

"When we entered the tunnel there was an enormous roar which shook the walls. In front of us a partition made of rocks collapsed, giving way to a beautiful train station. We followed Madison further along the train track until we came to an archway. There were clouds of dust and debris billowing out of it, as if there had been a minor earthquake or something. Once the dust had settled, giant boulders – which must have fallen from above – filled in what must have been the ravine."

"The roar you heard was from a dragon."

"Ha-ha. Oh . . . you're serious, aren't you?" Sam gulped.

"You wouldn't believe a word of what's happened down here," Olly said. "Even I'm still pinching myself. We've seen things which aren't from this world, from ghosts to creatures from the underworld. I'm so glad it's over."

Jessica laughed. "Well you might have been hallucinating, you have been down here a while!"

Sam tapped her on the shoulder. "I think we'd better start believing this stuff, look over there."

In the corner of the cave a haze appeared, which quickly turned into an apparition. "First you take our treasure, throw me to my death and now you try and kill my son!" the ghostly figure boomed out.

"Victor!" Orion shouted. "I could never forget that voice."

"Who?" Jess asked.

"It's Victor Golding; Marshall's dad. He and his brother kidnapped me a long time ago and took me into these caves."

"And now I'm back to help my son. You may think you've succeeded by killing Hornbeam, but I can bring back the creatures from the underworld."

Leo stood next to his dad and spoke with confidence. "The afterlife is no more in these caves. The underworld has reclaimed all the evil. Anyway, you're just a ghost, you can't hurt us!"

"Mwahahahaha!" Victor's ghost snarled. "My grandad took my brother and I to the Art of Darkness club and taught us what we needed to know. I could start hell on Earth if I wanted!"

The ghost raised its transparent arms, shut its eyes and chanted in a language unfamiliar to everyone in the cave.

"What the hell is going on?" Sam whispered, squeezing Jess's hand.

"I've no idea. Shall we all just get the heck out of here?"

"Hang on a sec," Olly said, watching Leo

rummaging through his rucksack. "What are you looking for?"

"This!" Leo replied, triumphantly.

In his hand was the cube that had held George Bumble's ghost a prisoner for many years. "You picked it up!" Olly said. "I thought we'd left it back at the station. Quick, can you translate the hieroglyphics?"

"I'll give it a go," Leo said, opening the box.

"Don't worry, I know," said Orion. "It was the first thing I remember hearing after being sedated."

As Leo held the box, Orion read out the phrase:

THIS WILL HOLD THE SPIRIT SAFE,
AWAY FROM THE ENTIRE HUMAN RACE.

A beam of light shot out of the cube and headed straight for Victor. Before the ghost had chance to finish off summoning the underworld, it was absorbed by the light and sucked into the cube.

"Got you!" Leo shouted, slamming the cube lid shut.

"You did it!" Olly said. "Even without your slayer powers, you are one brave lad."

"Well done, Son," Orion said as he welled up. "Your mother is going to be so proud of you."

"And she will be of you too, Dad!"

Everyone gave each other a big hug knowing they were finally free.

"So, what are we meant to do with him?" Jess said pointing down to Marshall who was still flat out on the floor.

"We'll tie his hands together using this," Leo said, pulling a length of rope out of his bag.

Olly laughed, "Bloomin' heck, mate, have you got the kitchen sink in there as well?"

"Ha-ha, well it's best to be prepared."

"True, mate. Anyway, let's get him tied, he'll start coming round soon. You hit him quite hard didn't you, Sis?"

"No one messes with my brother and gets away with it," Jess said, putting a comforting arm around him.

When Marshall regained consciousness, Sam and Orion picked him up off the floor. "Hey, what's going on?" he said, sounding drunk.

"Well, in a nutshell," Olly said, looking at him with

a large smile on his face, "You were hit on the head, had a visit from your dead dad and now we're taking you out of here to the police station, where you and your family belong."

"You what?" Marshall mumbled. "My dad was here?"

"He appeared as a ghost trying to help you, but it wasn't a problem for us. We've dealt with a lot worse than that in the last day or so."

Marshall slumped his head forward, knowing the game was up for him. Sam and Orion held an arm each and started walking him out of the caves. "It should be a lot easier getting out of here without those creatures trying to kill us all," Orion said, laughing.

"Sure will," said Leo. "Still can't believe I've found you after all these years. We've got so much to catch up on."

"I know, we're going to be a family again very soon."

They made their way through the cave system, shining torches in front of them. The glowing creatures that had previously guided their way may have disappeared, but the clever Labrador knew exactly which way they had come in.

As they came to the labyrinth caves, all was silent. There weren't any creatures or giant spiders chasing them, just empty caves. The noise from Hornbeam's roar had caused partial collapses, allowing them easy passage. On exiting the labyrinths, they came across one of the biggest obstacles they had faced when first entering the tunnels.

"Wow, I can't believe how much this has changed," Olly said, seeing the vast ravine filled with giant boulders."

"I know," Leo said. "Look Dad, that's where we had to swing over on a giant web . . . Dad?"

Orion was wiping tears from his eyes. "Sorry, it's just that the last time I was up here I fell down the ravine thinking I was going to die and would never see you and your mum again."

Leo walked over and gave him a cuddle. "I love you so much, Dad."

"Love you too, Leo. Come on, let's get the hell out of here."

They walked over the fallen boulders and on

through the archway leading to the train platform. In the far distance they could see a pinprick of light coming from the tunnel entrance. The partitioning wall had also given way.

"Not far now, everyone!" Jess encouraged. "By the way, there'll be a few people out there waiting for us. I took it on myself to ring the police and your parents before Sam and I entered the tunnel, just in case we needed help as well. Thought I'd better tell you now to lessen the shock, it's going to be a bit full on when we get outside."

"Can't believe my mum's out there," Leo said, his gentle walk increasing to a sprint until he was running at full speed towards the light.

"Be careful! Don't trip up!" Orion shouted.

Leo reached the tunnel exit and stepped out through the rusty metal sheets. The sun was shining brightly, causing him to raise his hand over his squinting eyes.

"Leo?" a familiar voice said.

Pulling his hand down, Leo gave his eyes a few seconds to adjust to the light. "Mum, Mum!" he shouted, focusing on the figure running toward him.

"I'm so glad you're all right. What on earth have you been up to? You were meant to be staying at your friend's house."

"It's a long story, but it'll become a lot clearer in a few minutes. Just look over there," Leo said, pointing to the exit.

The rest of the group were making their way out of the tunnel. First came Jess, Olly and the panting dog who were greeted by their parents. Then came Sam who was guiding a still disorientated Marshall over the metal barrier.

"Over here, officers!" Olly ordered. "We've made a citizen's arrest. This boy, James Golding Marshall, enticed Leo and I down here where he then tried to kill us. He would have succeeded as well if it wasn't for Jess and Sam."

"Don't forget Madison," Jess said.

"Woof!" she barked in reply.

"Oh, you need to find his Uncle Lance," Olly continued. "He kidnapped Leo's dad eleven years ago and he was the brains behind all of this."

One of the police officers stepped forward and spoke. "Well thank you, Olly for your enthusiasm in all this, but we do need evidence and will have to take statements from everyone here."

"Well you can start with interviewing me then," a voice came out of the tunnel.

Everyone looked over to see Orion striding out from the place which had kept him prisoner for all those years.

"Oh, my goodness. Orion? Is that really you?" Leo's mum shouted in disbelief.

"It sure is, Mel," Orion said, rushing over to hold his wife.

"I never thought I'd see you again, love."

"Seeing you again was the only thing that kept me alive down there. I would never have left you both on purpose, you know that."

Pushing his head between his parents, Leo cuddled into both bodies, putting his arms around them. "My family is finally back together."

"It sure is, Son, it sure is," Orion said, with a huge smile lighting up his worn and exhausted face.

Leaving his parents, Leo remembered something very important and wandered over to the police. "Before I forget, I've got something to give you guys."

Opening his rucksack, he grandly produced the cube. "I'm not going to explain what this is or what's in it. Mainly because you'll never believe me. But one thing's for sure, please keep it safe and never, ever open it."

"Don't worry, lad, we'll keep it under lock and key until the investigation's all finished."

The officers shuffled everyone into their vans and took them to the nearest station for questioning. Over many hours, stories about dragons and creatures from the underworld fell on to deaf ears. Thankfully they did realise Orion had been kidnapped by Lance and forced down the tunnel. They also searched Marshall's home and discovered the plans detailing how to kill everyone and steal the treasure. The police were also provided with information on the past disappearance of George Bumble and how he was murdered by the now deceased Drake Golding.

It didn't take long for a jury to find Lance Golding and his nephew, James Golding Marshall, guilty of kidnapping and attempted murder. Lance was sentenced to life with a minimum term of ten years in H.M.P. Northallerton and Marshall was detained for public protection for a minimum term of ten years at Wetherby Young Offenders Institute.

George Bumble was remembered with a posthumous medal for bravery and for his efforts to keep the treasure for the town of Brunswick.

Eventually, the tunnel was condemned as a health and safety hazard, with the entrance being bricked up. Although there were rumours that it could be opened again and made into a tourist attraction.

The jewels and precious stones had been removed from the treasure cave and were now safely housed in the Brunswick Museum in a new exhibition focusing on the stories and myths of what may have happened down in the dark depths. These included the story of George Bumble's dream of creating an amazing attraction, his bravery medal, the bow and arrows which were found down there, a few swords, and Marshall's gun.

But the most interesting object was the cube, kept in the centre of the room in a glass dome. Nobody really believed the stories of what had happened down in the caves beneath the town of Brunswick, but people did seem scared of the cube. It apparently held the ghost of Victor Golding.

The exhibition was a huge success, attracting visitors from miles around. One keenly inquisitive child whispered, "Mummy, I'm sure I just saw that cube move."

THE END

If you enjoyed *The Search for Orion*, please consider leaving a review on Amazon and Goodreads – these can make all the difference to an author and help other readers to find and enjoy the book.

Thank you.

ACKNOWLEDGEMENTS

First of all, I would like to thank Time. Believe me, I've needed a lot of it. Without this, my story could not and would not have nurtured itself into what it has become today.

I would like to thank Louise Burke for editing my story and to Karen Perkins for her editing and general help in getting me started on the road to publication.

Finally, a massive thank you to my wife Melanie Corneby-Robinson and my son Ryan, for putting up with me through my ups and downs of writing this book. It's been a long road, but I've reached my destination.

ABOUT THE AUTHOR

Keith Robinson – writing as Keith Cador – was born in 1975 in the spa town of Harrogate, North Yorkshire. He now lives in the City of Ripon, North Yorkshire, with his wife Melanie and son Ryan.

This is his debut novel, which is the first in The Art of Darkness series, where he's taken his own memories of growing up and transformed them into a mythical children's adventure.

Printed in Great Britain
by Amazon